Waggle

Waggle

a novel

Joe Redden Tigan

iUniverse, Inc.
New York Lincoln Shanghai

Waggle

iUniverse books may be ordered through booksellers or by contacting:

iUniverse
2021 Pine Lake Road, Suite 100
Lincoln, NE 68512
www.iuniverse.com
1-800-Authors (1-800-288-4677)

This is a work of fiction. All of the characters, names, incidents, organizations, and dialogue in this novel are either the products of the author's imagination or are used fictitiously.

ISBN-13: 978-0-595-41619-6 (pbk)
ISBN-13: 978-0-595-85969-6 (ebk)
ISBN-10: 0-595-41619-5 (pbk)
ISBN-10: 0-595-85969-0 (ebk)

Printed in the United States of America

To Mom and Dad

There is the man *and* his virtues.
                              —Emerson

The 1st hole at Triple-the-Pines Golf Course is known as The Noose, a daunting array of water, sand, trees, and penal gorse-like rough. Emphasis on penal. Dense forest and gorse-like rough intimidate the fairway from each side, the fairway itself being the width of the shoulder on an Illinois country road.

—*Chicago Golf*

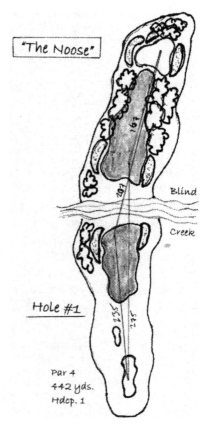

"The Noose"

Blind

Creek

Hole #1

Par 4
442 yds.
Hdcp. 1

On July 28, 2003, it was 72°F and mostly sunny in Carlsburg, Illinois. It's on record with the *Keefe County Chronicle*. Winds were calm at 3-5 MPH and the dewpoint stood at 49°F, which, that's a ridiculously low dewpoint for late July around here. It indicates that there was very little humidity, as dewpoints measure the air's capacity to hold water vapor in places like jungles and the Midwest during summer.

Conny Bromenn sat behind his desk, breathing easily, his shoulder to the 8 AM light of the windows that are in the east wall of his living room. Conny's early 1900s brick bungalow is located on the west side of Carlsburg just off that side's official historic district line. Some crops had been about a half-mile southwest of his house, but the southwest was now under siege of course since it was, after all, an open area. It was a daily dust storm during that July where when the dust settled over the southwest at night and upon waking up the next day a new giant warehouse was visible or "townhomes" to either side of the warehouses appeared, or a new hotel, all looking like a prepos-terously boring erector set on the horizon where pieces had been clipped on without error. In his bungalow, Conny's living room had all its original wood trim exposed, and Conny and the wood sat there all smothered just then in aurae. The aurae, they mixed like cream.

There was an air cooler than room temperature but not cold trying the sills of Conny's open windows. He opened the desk drawer that held the telephone books and scraps of paper, the wooden drawer opening and closing so easily now in the vastness of a 49°F-dewpoint comfort level. Conny had to repeat the action of opening and closing it a couple more times, each time faster and with more emphasis on the slide, so that the improved con-ductivity of the telephone book drawer did in fact directly affect his stamen stronger and better than each slide before.

Nothing affects my stamen more than comfort, Conny thought. *Nothing.*

Carlsburg itself has only recently qualified as being part of Chicagoland because of its death-defyingly unbridled approach to commercial and residential real estate development. In an attempt to grow the county at a rate 14 times the national aver-age, which is a lot, Keefe County zoning officials have defined and then redefined suburban sprawl by paving three quarters of a county in about a year and a half that beforehand was primarily agricultural and quiet and pretty, and *quiet*. This made Keefe County appalling overnight and, hence, endeared itself to the original Chicagoland counties of Cook, DuPage, and parts of Will and Lake, the "collar" counties of Chicago, which have been good and paved and appalling for a while now. Keefe County paved anything that hadn't been paved yet (or was paved once but had crumbled) between it and Chicagoland. It informally annexed itself to Chicagoland without having to endure the kind of red tape that can come from formally annexing things. Instead, it needed only to cover about 160,000 square acres of farm, forest, and wetlands with malls, gas stations, and residential subdivisions, each with plenty of roads and in-roads that are almost completely ineffective in actually guiding the abundant traffic. If Conny, for example, were to drive "out" to places where he used to get high and drink beer back in high school, he'd be standing in the middle of a superstore that was surrounded by superstores and stores and restaurants, their space of which is quadrupled by their parking space that still doesn't offer enough space for parking.

As luck would have it, however, a considerable part of this development and revenue generation has been *golf*. Also luckily, they have not yet decided to play golf on a paved surface, which, you can't rule it out, given the bloodlust for trajectory and length and amassing as many yds. per shot as possible since it's all about height and distance and torque these days. What better element than pavement for inducing more of all that? Add to that the simple fact that we're running out of unpaved land.

But on a day that is 72°F and mostly sunny—at least for those playing golf on that day—Chicagoland could be a Paradise not lost so much as maybe just confused about which way to go.

July 28, 2003 was a weekday, a Mon., and it would start out like days from a not too distant past, the kind of days that people pine about with the unique emotional conflict that comes specifically from pining about those kinds of days from the not too distant past, that unique conflict resulting from real determination to return to those days someday combined with the utter futility of ever being able to stop the gut-wrenchingly relentless development in order to do so. To return. Quiet, July 28, 2003 started out as, with the pace that comes from walking or at least witnessing people walk, and it had a sense the day did of possibly being able to offer humans the chance to actually control what their next move might be.

The air and the aurae were piercing the prior day's humid malaise and flushing the beleaguering heat and humidity from around Conny. Ideas were surfacing then subsiding, and Conny let them bubble freely and disperse of their own accordance. Conny didn't fear reflection that morning. Some ideas appeared with titles, some with faces. Some appeared as spreadsheets.

Conny was strong as he ever was just then, the aurae a cream-foam froth over his epidermis and causing effervescence in what he thought would technically be known as his cranium and with a direct link to what he knew for sure was his stamen. A voltage that made him feel so much better to the point that he wondered if a seizure could be all that far behind. Conny had then the combined strengths of the inflated clean-and-jerk artist and of the wiry yogi master.

The time to break 75 is now. That's what Conny was thinking.

He thought that the feeling of being outside on a day that is biologically perfect to human beings—simply standing outside somewhere—is the greatest true feeling possible. The greatest true feeling possible for humans. It is sunny for our human perspective, with only occasional cumulus clouds to please our eyes and promote our imagination, and it's about 72°F, with no variance readings from any weather indices meaning the day is without humidity or some second source of heat we as humans can't seem to pinpoint so we invented a heat *index* to try to measure it.

Trees are not humid blue but are actually green and bright green. That feeling—where mechanisms for human body temperature control are seated comfortably in a chair out in the breeze, blood-flow through the skin and subcutaneous area never had it so easy, the mere thought of vasoconstriction is a joke on a day like this, and breathing in normally is downright spiritual—that feeling is the greatest feeling we can achieve as humans without requiring interference, like drugs, other humans, or mechanical propulsion, for examples. So, what is the prospect of a game of *golf* on a day like this?

Conny contemplated this, aware that he was contemplating and appreciating the ability to do so, drawer in hand.

This 519-yd. par-5 opens itself up in welcome relief from Hole 1's Noose. This is the only par-5 at Triple-the-Pines that can be reachable in two for the bigger hitters. Originally a much tighter hole than it is now, Hole 2 was almost immediately altered after its inception so as to give players a second chance after visiting The Noose. A reason to go on.

—*Chicago Golf*

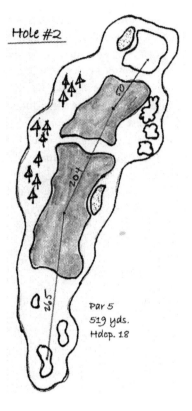

Hole #2

Par 5
519 yds.
Hdcp. 18

Given that the previous week had been in the 90s but was still remembered more for its debilitating blue haze of humidity than for its very high temperatures, July 28, 2003 didn't just dawn: A goddess of the sky and the very personification of the dawn of the Earth's morning heralded it in. A fresh breeze was felt at her approach and when the first rays of the morning sun touched her face, the goddess gave forth a sound like the arpeggio of dulcimer strings. All species stopped and took note of it in unison. Plants, animals, and humans were brethren overwhelmed by the miracle of nature in Chicagoland on July 28, 2003. Worms surfaced just from the rumors. They all soon moved on in their own ways, but each happier for a reprieve from the clammy brutality of Chicagoland near the end of July, for having socked away a glimpse of everything around them in supreme clarity, however briefly that would be afforded.

For Constantine Bromenn, the way of moving on that day was to first initiate a tee time at Triple-the-Pines Golf Course, then find the willing players. Conny thought about them. He thought:

> **Clark Sweet is probably an 11-handicapper and a respectable player with what isn't the worst swing in the world, though he's a liar when he says he's a 7-handicapper.**
>
> **Residence: Carlsburg, IL (12 years)**
> **Age: 40**
> **Occupation: Mortgage Broker, DuKeefe Mortgage Corp.**

> Clark Sweet is an horrific liar. A self-proclaimed 7-handicapper who enters false scores into the pro shop's handicap indexing machine after each round and sometimes for "ghost rounds," Clark Bar's 18 holes are always complicated by the inexplicable, especially for a 7-handicapper:

>> "How can you make *double* bogey on a hole with no hazards?" and

>> "How do you find the rough on a fairway this *wide*?" and

>> "How does that putt *not* break right?" and

"Are you kidding me—a gust of wind *just* as my ball gets up in the air?" in constant wind and

"Wow, that *shot* sure felt better than that *result* …" and the occasional, disgustedly blunt

"Jesus, Sweet."

And what has become an inevitable payout in the clubhouse after losing badly in a Nassau wager because his handicap is too damn low to suit his actual talent.

Conny reminded himself that:

While the Nassau can be played as a team game, it's more often employed as an individual contest, and is really three separate bets, those being for the best score for the front-9, best score for the back-9, and best total score for the 18 holes, and where:

1. the front-9 is given a value in dollars, and

2. the back-9 is given a value in dollars, and

3. the total-18 is given a value in dollars, (*NOTE: any values can be given by the players, except by Buck O'Royerson*) and

4. whoever has the best score for the front-9 wins the front, best score for the back-9 wins the back, and best score for the total-18 wins the 18. Winning the trifecta can induce giddiness in veterans of war.

Conny tried but could not remember the last time he saw Sweet break 85. There was that round up in Wisconsin at Presswood G.C. about four years ago when Sweet shot 80 one time after finding out that Ron Ruthke, the Midwest Regional Finance Director at DuKeefe Mortgage—and Sweet's direct boss—had been fired for "misappropriation or malappropriation or misfeasance or malfeasance or whatever" as Sweet described it. Fresh off the good news (which, it was good because 1) Ron was Sweet's boss and, as a boss, he was a "complete" dick and did not understand any of either "the basics" or "people" and so his departure was a necessary cutting of dead weight, a thinning of the herd, and would herald in a new start of unlimited potential not just for Sweet's division but for the entire company because "Hey, it's like a domino effect" and 2) it meant Sweet took over Ron's job), Clark Bar couldn't contain his game and it's often unexpressed verve, and shot 80 very easily. The usual 3-putts were the only way he left some strokes out there. But Conny hadn't seen game like that from Sweet since.

It would be unfair to say that a 79 didn't maybe lurk in Clark Bar; it just very, very rarely surfaced. Or as Buck O'Royerson once put it, "Sweet is Loch Ness and 79 is the Monster."

Conny remembered that:

Also: What isn't so simple is how certain players in a foursome will choose to contend in a Nassau with each other. The Nassau is often a side bet amongst individuals that accompanies the team Scotch game (or other team games) and it can be a real gonads-reconfiguring game the Nassau can, shining a spotlight on the proclaimed strength/handicap of a golfer's game/honor and its sharp contrast to reality in many instances. You have only your own scoring ability as a golfer to rely on in the Nassau, and that ability is in direct relation to your handicap maintenance, so basically, the Nassau is like the truth. It also has an interesting way of allowing players to personalize their intense competition with other select players. For example, one time a couple of summers ago, Buck O'Royerson, in a rare fit of sobriety, had a calm night before a Sat. morning tee time and he got to the course about an hour early, had orange juice and a banana, spent that early time hitting golf balls on the range and in the process figured out a swing mechanic that had been preventing him from enjoying golf for about six months. Buck then went to the putting green with the intention of hitting only three putts because his putter was merely an extension of his hands for some reason that morning and he wasn't going to fuck that up by "confusing the issue with practice." There, he briefly overheard Clark Bar explaining to some guys the subtleties of the 74 he fired the other day in 30 MPH winds. Problem with that is, Buck was there that particular day with Sweet and no matter how drunk Buck was, he knows Sweet shot 84 at best in those 30 MPH winds, and so upon gathering at the 1st tee, in front of Conny and Bob Van Worthington, Buck challenged Sweet and only Sweet to a $50-$50-$100 Nassau with the option to press (double) the back-9 and total-18, all of which is a good reason why Buck doesn't get to place values in a Nassau wager anymore, even sober—and maybe especially so.

Tom Blair is probably a 13-handicapper based on rounds actually finished, with a good swing and excellent knowledge of course management, ironically.

Residence: Carlsburg, IL (8 years)
Age: 41
Occupation: Real Estate Appraiser (independent)

Tom Blair is known for being a wife's husband. That is, he's known equally as "Jennie's husband" as he is Tom Blair. Rarely allowed to run totally free on the golf course, Blurry must often stealth-golf since he is either being clocked by his wife at home and needs to finish his round sooner than is ever realistically plausible, or he is there completely against her will, or lies to her flat out and says he is someplace else, which is notably unsuccessful on beautiful days in Chicagoland. In fact, while it is rare, it is not unheard of for Blurry to leave his foursome and join the group ahead if they are three or less, and even leave that group if a group ahead is also three or less, in order to sort of career himself across the 18 holes to finish quickly and avoid home-style wrath. If a particularly threatening call should come over his ever present cell phone, Blurry is doe-like in traversing the woods (where he considerately takes his calls) and completing the hole and telling guys he really needs to move ahead, joining the group in front. Blurry can be so doe-like, in fact, that on one occasion about two years ago, O'Royerson, having come that morning straight from a bar that a friend owns and having sampled the latest version of street-grade mushroom that was being passed around, had the opportunity to be playing with Blurry when Blurry needed to run the gauntlet. The call came from Jennie at a particular vantage point on the back-9 at Triple-the-Pines that offered a complete, unobstructed vista of Blurry's run, and while drunk and sort of skunked on some primo "FUN-gus," O'Royerson was able to observe the little marathon and perceived Blurry to be a scared rabbit, meaning he thought Blurry was a *rabbit* for a minute, then went on to par the 12th hole the way Buck does sometimes. Which, a rabbit isn't a doe, but they're no that far apart as far as O'Royerson is concerned, especially when goofed on some rather bodacious shroomage.

Blurry's like the portrayal of a golf husband in a mediocre movie about the difficulties men have committing and don't know how they'll ever give up their freedom for things like golf, hanging with their buddies, and having sex, meaningless sex, with other women. Except Blurry's totally committed to his wife, she makes damn sure, hence the Herculean effort to convince her he's either not on the golf course, or he is but he's not having fun, can't have fun without her, and so will definitely have no problem being home in the allotted time. "Nope, I won't even feel like a beer after the round, honey" Blurry has said during many a cell phone conversation from the 18th tee before many a tense beer after the round.

Considering the pressure, no one can figure out why Blurry leaves his cell phone on during a round, and furthermore, why he answers it when he has full knowledge of who is calling and what for. He knows he can't hide the fact that he's on a golf course given the particular sounds that nature and men playing golf in the background make together. Guys used to try to help Blurry out by muffling themselves when he picked up the phone, but after only so long of enduring how he has lied to his wife about golfing and then answers his cell anyway when he knows it's her, guys sort of said *fuck it*. You could tell who Blurry's best friends were by observing the seemingly disproportionate relationship between the amount of time afforded Blurry before the "fuck it" approach was enacted and those who enacted it, with the best friends allowing the least amount of time to cut Blurry some slack before thinking *fuck it*. People with good friends understand how this is actually proportionate, though.

With that much distraction involved, one might think how the hell does he ever get invited to play, but Blurry's actually a pretty solid ball striker who's been playing a fairly long time, he did take the game up pre-Tiger Woods, and he knows all the money games so you don't have to explain them and is steadfast about etiquette, aside from the occasional but sometimes horrifically awkward conversations with his wife over the phone. It's gotten to the point where a tradition has developed where anytime Blurry tries to enact the rules of golf (e.g., telling Buck he can't move his ball after Buck moves a ball out of a divot hole on the 16th fairway and declares it "ground under repair" because he rarely gets a nice drive on the 16th for some reason and the one time he does it winds up in a freaking divot hole of course and he just can't take it), Buck likes to remind Blurry that CDGA (Chicago District Golf Association) tournament rules stipulate: "The use of a cellular phone, pager, or any other portable electronic communication device by a contestant or caddie during a round is strictly prohibited. Penalty for breach of the policy is immediate disqualification. The CDGA defines 'use' as having the device in one's possession while it is powered on." Buck is often congratulated for having memorized the passage so accurately.

Conny considered that:

Also: It's not that other guys don't have wives and children and in-laws and pets; most of them do. They just aren't caricatures of the husband sneaking around on his wife (to play golf), nor are the wives caricatures of the ball-and-chain at home; the brooding golf widow. Either that or they were caricatures at one time, but through the kind of repetition that is associated with terms like "bombardment" and "head against a brick wall" they succumbed to the reality of the golf situation and knew they could no longer exist as a caricature and still maintain their credibility and sanity, or at least open the door to the possibility of happiness occurring on Sat. mornings, regardless. So their caricatures faded away, and each wife and husband experienced their own private and very memorable moment when they decided the golf situation was part of the nature of things and they were just getting older. Not Blurry's Jennie, though. She would not go gentle into that Sat. morning. She would, in fact, rage. But Blurry'll go to the woods or wherever for his talks with her and still manage to maintain proper pace of play, most of the time, with one foursome or another.

Bob Van Worthington's handicap is indeterminable, but he lies and cheats and plays to a 15 with an unnatural swing and what looks to be severe discomfort walking after about 8 holes.

Residence: South Halcyon, IL (6 years)
Age: 42
Occupation: Real Estate Appraiser (independent)

Robert Van Worthington is an unholy cheat. The thing about Not Worthy is the very scariest thing in golf. The cheating. And not in universally acceptable ways. Not Worthy is not beyond literally plucking a ball with his fingers from bad lies in tall rough (or let's face it, any lie that simply doesn't look right) in attempts to ameliorate his own situation. Not Worthy cheats so much that in the clubhouse, even after a few beers and after Bob has left, guys still can't estimate exactly how many strokes should be added to his score based on some of the shit he pulled out there.

Bob's nickname—while kept secret from him and not just for obvious reasons but also because he remains distant enough from other guys so as not to have the comfort level required to call him Not Worthy to his face—was concocted during a freak accident: While playing Triple-the-Pines's back-9 about three years ago with Conny and Clark Bar and Ethan Wagner, the youngster who worked the driving range, their foursome approached the difficult 13th hole, a 195-yd. par-3 slightly uphill demon with a bit of a crowned green surrounded by traps left and right and Black's Bog back and left. (The wetland's sobriquet was derived from Triple-the-Pines's current and only greenskeeper, Phil Black, sliding a front-end loader back-asswards into the marshy "terra-apparently-not-very-firma" during a midnight attempt to complete a sand trap along the 12th hole). Not Worthy selected a spot between the tee markers, squatted with the lack of balance telling of his poor coordination and how it/he was being toyed with by the wind that day, implanted tee and ball into the ground, and wavered back up squinting into the wind and ailing from walking more than 8 holes. Picking his 3-wood directly up off the ground and coiling his shoulder turn in a way so deliberate you might think he was hoisting groceries from the trunk of his car, Bob made his painful swing at that time completely fazed by the wind and possibly with no knowledge of what the ball looked like below him, and struck the ball at its equator with a small part of the bottom quarter of his 3-wood. He could have missed the ball entirely so many different ways that Sweet would later proclaim during a rain delay that he fully intended to draw up schematics of Not Worthy's swing from the 13th tee that day and contact the physics folks at Fastlab National Accelerator Laboratory (where they discovered the bottom quark, the top quark, and the tau neutrino, all right there in the western suburbs of Chicago), to find out if, given the circumstances, a finite number could actually be placed on how many ways Bob could have completely missed the ball, fully expecting to hear back from Fastlab that, no, after three weeks of research, a finite number could not be ascertained. The possibilities were endless. Thing is, Bob didn't miss completely. His ball flew for about 50 of the 195 yds. required to reach the hole. From there, Bob's ball did not behave like a round object in the least and, even in the wind, Conny and Sweet would both say later that they heard it make a funny *sound*, too, the ball making jagged leaps and hisses as though the ground were intensely hot and the ball couldn't stand it to land anywhere, until the last 25 yds. of its odyssey when, with locked and unmistakable precision, it cooled down, slowed down, and as gingerly as a cat burglar atop autumns' first frost one might say, found the bottom of the hole like a 2 ½-ft. putt in the hands of Ben Crenshaw. While trying to figure out what it was that they had just witnessed, Ethan Wagner dropped to his knees and chanted "We're not worthy! We're not worthy!"

That night in Sweet's basement, Conny and Sweet would use some free time to review many of the ways that Bob *was* Not Worthy, not the least of which was his hole-in-one, and maybe the most of which was the fact that he was such an unholy cheat, and they would propagate the nickname via other guys, who have miraculously kept it from earshot of Bob, even when drinking.

Conny reconsidered that:

Also: It comes up for debate a lot amongst guys, and their conclusion or as close to a conclusion as they'll ever get to one is that Not Worthy differs from Clark

Bar in that he lies and cheats about what he's doing *while* he's doing it with total abandonment and an unscrupulous, gouging bent towards manipulating his score as it directly relates to the money game, whereas Sweet takes whatever punishment the foursome can dish out then just lies to himself/the CDGA later about his talent. That's not to condone what Sweet does any more than Not Worthy. The kind of self-absorption required to make sure you stay a single-digit handicapper (mid-range single digits, to boot) regardless of having not broken 85 in four years, and not having ever done it that much prior to four years ago, borders on the pathological if it doesn't actually reside there, plus it's flat out delusional. If Clark Bar didn't have diversions as meaty as a family and a job, there would be reason to worry, given his aptitude for delusion.

Buck O'Royerson is about a 10-hadicapper, but who knows what he could play to sober. (Better or worse, guys often debate.)

Residence: Carlsburg, IL (33 years)
Age: 40
Occupation: Real Estate Appraiser (independent)

William "Buck" O'Royerson is a gambler. An addict. There are several bona fide ways to gamble while playing golf, but guys can count on Buck to introduce a new money game every now and then that richly explores the relationship between gambling and the natural parameters of golf. For example, one time about four years ago, Buck showed up for a 7:37 AM Sat. tee time having come straight from the casino boat "docked" on Pentwater River in Halcyon, Keefe County, reeking of mixed boozes and looking yellow and brown in areas that are usually more caucasiatic on Buck and unexpectedly finding $400 in his shirt pocket when paying greens fees. It would be discovered later that Buck had actually spent about 20 hours on the boat, somewhere near the end of which he purchased a sportshirt and shorts from the casino gift shop to try to suit his impending golf game, each embroidered strategically near a pocket with *Rollin' (The Dice) On The River? You Bet!!* with arrows on each side of the slogan pointing to the pocket lip. Buck approached his group on the 1st tee with no time to spare proclaiming he had the best money game in town and calling Conny "Richard" as he glided by him quickly even though he's known Conny since junior high. He told Clark Bar that he was going to have to "double down today, Dorothy," which Sweet couldn't tell if that had some relation to Buck's new money game (which, OK by Sweet) or if it was simply a sentiment from last night that was still making a lasting impression on Buck this morning for some reason. As rocked as he was, Buck could still make a reliable swing at the ball because he was such a practiced drinker and the type of guy that got partially *anchored* by a day and half of booze, if you can imagine it—he would fall asleep before his swing truly gave out on him—which, when Not Worthy witnessed this in Buck for the first time, he became preoccupied for the next three days by the role fate plays in our lives, especially as far as who gets to be coordinated and who doesn't is concerned. After getting off the first tee inconspicuously enough, Buck had the foursome sold on his new money game by the time they reached their approach shots, explaining the rules enthusiastically and exclaiming "Double down, ladies!" at the end of each rule even though it still remained to be seen if there was any way of doubling down in this game, as it were, or if there was even any way to employ the term "double down" metaphorically, like sportsmen might. Here's what was employed:

1. The ability to roll your ball to the fairway if you are within one foot of it in the secondary (shorter) cut of rough.

2. The ability to roll the ball into the secondary cut of rough if you are within one foot of it in the primary (taller) cut of rough.

3. If par (handicaps NOT considered) was *not* made after choosing to improve your lie from the *secondary* cut of rough to the *fairway*, the player improving his lie paid *each* man the value of whatever number hole the group is on at that time. E.g., one time on the 14th hole Buck liked his chances and moved his ball from the secondary cut of rough to the fairway but double-bogeyed after suddenly running short on beer, so he paid out $14 to each man = $42.

4. The ability of a *non-lie-improving* player to bet the value of a hole *against* the *lie-improving player*, regardless of which cut of rough he improves from, with the non-lie-improving player:

   a. paying the value of the hole to each man in the foursome if par is made by the lie-improving player, and

   b. *double* the value if birdie is made, which, that still has no relation to how someone would double down in Black Jack for a number of reasons, but at least there's a "double" in there somewhere and possibly lessened the degree to which Buck was drunk and lent the group a little comfort that maybe he would in fact not fall asleep before the round is over; not that it's happened before, but like they all said to each other as Buck approached them on the first tee that morning, "My God, look at him," and

c. receiving the value of the hole from each player for a score worse than par by the lie-improving player, which:

　　i. puts pressure enough on the lie-improving player to cause him to jerk, and

　　ii. makes everyone think real hard about improving their lie (especially on the back-9) though the temptation to do so is oftentimes breathtaking.

5. The ability of the *lie-improving player* to bet on his *own* chances of making par or better, which doubles everything in #4 (only in reverse) and, finally, represents a self-imposed doubling down of some sort.

It's interesting to note in area 4.c. of Buck's game that the guys very quickly picked up on a loophole that could negate paying out to a non-lie-improving player who bet against the lie-improving player, and that would be by making sure all three non-lie-improving players made the same bet against the lie-improving player. That way, when par was not made, as it often is not, bets were negated except for the lie-improving player, who paid the value of the hole to the other three men after not making par. It was shameless of course, and worked quite well until Blurry improved his lie from the secondary cut of rough to the fairway on the 12th hole not only to improve his lie but also because moving the ball one foot would legally take him out from behind a tree, and Buck bet against his making par since Blurry had not made a par yet that day, and Conny and Sweet followed suit. Problem with that being Blurry hit the greatest 7-iron of his entire life into the green, landing less than a foot from the cup, Blurry pulling a natural birdie out of his ass, forcing the three scheisters to each pay him $24 and obliterating the former loophole.

Though Buck's original name for this game was *Roll It Over In The Clover*, it would quickly become known as *Double Down!* to the rest of the group that day.

Conny recalled that:

Also: Even though guys will do anything to rip apart the other's pride and wallet and preferably in that order, they could sometimes show signs that there was hope for civilization in Carlsburg. During Buck's game and as regaled later by Buck himself, regardless of the circumstances it was "heartening, to say the least" to see that no one disagreed on how to measure the distance of one foot without the benefit of a tape measure or anyone with a size-12 shoe; an eyeballing was sufficient and no one raised too much hell about it, which was so astounding that someone went through the trouble of somehow accessing the dusty typewriter in Ken Blankenship's office at Triple-the-Pines and typing up a notice about it and posting it anonymously to the corkboard near the coffee machine. It read:

> *"We are from a tee time that is close to the 7:37 Sat. morning tee time, and we would like to commend that tee time for it's ability to agree. To maintain our anonymity, we won't say what our tee time is, but it was incredible to watch the 7:37 tee time's game unfold in*

front of us and not have our pace of play slowed down one bit. Not one bit. It was incredible, quite honestly. We ourselves have often thought that the rule against improving the lie of the ball in golf is often over-indulged, and we look forward to participating in what-ever game that was that the 7:37 tee time was playing that allows you to move your ball.

Well done, 7:37 tee time.

—Anon."

Despite that glowing report, Pogo Foley, the diminutive assistant pro at Triple-the-Pines, would later relate how he fielded several complaints about 7:37's pace of play via walkie-talkie from all of the elderly rangers (who monitored pace of play from carts with small awnings on which COURSE AMBASSADOR had been scripted) and from players who apparently had "found" unattended walkie-talkies of ambassadors. Many rangers and players alike mentioned the ability of their grandmothers to play faster than the 7:37 tee time, and some of their grandmothers were dead of course. Pogo would also relate how he occasionally glanced out the generous windows of the clubhouse that afford a panoramic view of the course to see if Buck had collapsed or something, but always seemed to catch the foursome in an odd dynamic where there were three guys practically standing over the fourth guy as he played his shot always from somewhere near the secondary cut of rough. *Another one of Buck's fucked up money games*, Pogo thought.

Bill Simons's handicap is about a 14, and a very able golfer at that but so full of shit that guys can sometimes hardly take it, even as full of shit as they themselves can often be.

Residence: Carlsburg, IL (5 years)
Age: 43
Occupation: Real Estate Appraiser (independent)

William Simons pretends to be a gambler and to know about gambling. Simons Says secretly and very deeply hates Bill O'Royerson, because Buck is the fleshy aromatic turbulent truth that outshines, however addicted and unwittingly, what Simons fashions himself as and has fashioned himself as for as long as guys have known him, but have never witnessed in him. Guys are skeptical of Simons Says's chronicles of all-night casino rolls, back-room hookers, and general law evadement. Such behavior certainly wasn't prevalent on the golf course, as was made shockingly apparent about three summers ago when Simons partnered with Sweet in a Scotch game against Conny and Buck.

Conny reminded himself that:
Though it can vary, the Scotch game as a lot of guys play it is a "points" game in which:

1. A foursome will be constructed of two teams.
2. Teams face off to see which can accumulate the most points per hole by getting:
    a. The lowest individual score (or *Ball*—short for low ball per hole).
    b. Lowest team score (or *Total*—short for lowest team total score per hole).

c. Closest to the pin in regulation (or *Prox*, or *Proxie*, which is short for closest proximity to the hole in regulation).

d. Birdie (*Birdie*—1 stroke under par for a hole).

These construct a 4-point game.

3. A team that is trailing (or "down") can "press" the bet, which is to double it, and should the lead change hands, the new trailing team can re-press, which in most places doubles the pressed amount, but some more conservative guys will just add the starting amount of the original bet to each press and re-press.

4. If a team garners *all* four points on *one* hole, they have achieved an "umbrella" and a kind of orgasm since that is:

a. A doubling of the points for that hole, or 4 = 8. (The term "umbrella" denotes that every possible thing has been "covered," like an umbrella policy for insurance coverage, coverage that goes beyond the scope of the underlying coverage. An umbrella becomes really interesting if presses are involved, obviously, since an *umbrella* on a *pressed* hole means the hole went from the value of 4 [original] = 8 [umbrella] = 16 [press], which could even be doubled again depending on how many presses guys allow per round. Put it this way: A lot of times, guys forget to designate on the 1st tee how many presses are allowed along with many other rules to many other games. So when O'Royerson, for example, presses for the fourth time just on the back-9 because he's $100 in the hole, numbers of presses allowed can become a bit of a point of argument you might say, particularly if points are valued at a dollar or above, which happens. Granted, you can only press when you're down, so it's not like you can run the table, sort of. But if you bump it 4 times quickly like that, keeping in mind that a press is not limited to just that hole but lasts throughout the rest of the 9-hole side and also reiterating that presses are *exponential*, not *multiple* [so a fourth press would mean $1 \neq 4$, but $1 = 16$], then, when O'Royerson has pressed you for the fourth time on the 14th hole, which he always seems to par come hell or high water, not only are points on the 14th worth $1 = 16$, but an *umbrella* mean $4 = 8 \times 16 = 128$. It also means that guys will actually get a picture of their paycheck stub and explanations to the family at dinnertime in their minds. *And* each of the remaining four holes would have this potential as well, meaning O'Royerson has finally reached the desperately sought euphoria of the addict, which, OK by Buck, but the numbers can start to become a little foreign to guys whose idea of a Tuesday night may *not* be chartering a plane out of Palwaukee Airport to Winnemucca Indian Reservation's Win-A-Buck-A Casino up in Wisconsin with $2,000 in tow just to see what happens.)

b. A very rare occurrence.

c. A real shaft-application to the pride and wallet of the other team—the Holy Grail, indeed.

Anyway, with Simons and Sweet up about 25 points after the 9th hole with points valued at a dollar for some daring reason in the Scotch game that morning three summers ago, and Buck being hung over, playing poorly, beginning to drink magnificent Old Styles, and generally unpredictable, Buck of course wanted to press on the 10th tee. Conny wasn't going to try to stop him. In a moment of weakness where the true cautious Simons bubbled beneath the thin and dissolving veneer of a wannabe gambler who wasn't an addict and was in the heat of the unexpected large lead with still a lot of golf left to be played, there was a brief silence after Buck requested just the *first* press of the round, as though Simons had forgotten in the midst of this … winning … that Buck could do that, he could *press*. Buck's press was immediately rejected by Simons Says, and without consultation with his partner, but with:

> "No fucking way!" and with a bit of a shake and a watering of just his left eye. Sweet audibly laughed at his own partner.

Conny remembered:

Also: A little known fact about presses: The team being pressed has the option of turning it down. *No fucking way!* aside, they can vote "no." There are a lot of guys in their 30s, 40s, and 50s who have taken the game up later in life and especially lately in the Tiger Woods Era who may not know that they have that option. Many times, they have just learned what a press is. Turning down a press is a little-known option also because if a guy turns down the press, well, you could cut the ridicule with a knife, so it rarely, rarely happens. In fact, the only possible version of a turned-down press would be something fully smart-assed. Like one time about a year and a half ago, Buck, teamed with Conny and frothing at the mouth for the opportunity to kick the numbers up, challenged Blurry and Sweet's team with a fifth and final press on the 18th hole making it worth crazy messed up money. Clark Bar saw the barbaric Celtic ancestry in Buck's eyes and the frothing of his mouth and the general twitching from stimulus overload that meant Buck was so very close to reaching the euphoria of the addict, which is when he's apparently furthest away from actually getting the euphoria according to some studies on addiction. If he could just be granted this fifth and final press, and Clark Bar knew it and knew about the studies and said he didn't really think a press would be prudent at this juncture. O'Royerson barked and told Sweet to drop his pants, he needed to prove that he was a man and Clark Bar said he was a man alright and with 90 of O'Royerson's dollars already so what on God's green earth did he need to accept another press for with just one hole left to play, but did.

It was still early enough that morning that the monstrous development had not yet begun to savage the town or countryside, the silence only enhancing Conny's intense regained ability to focus. His abundant powers of concentration hungered for subject matter. They manifested themselves in a daydream about his days playing golf on his first golf course, Outta-Matic G.C. "Outta-Matic" is the local dissolution of the proud albeit too damn foreign Outagamis name, and Outta-Matic is used even though the Carlsburg Park District has attempted French-Indian phonetics with its "Outta-Gah-Mee Golf Course" sign. Outta-Matic is a real throwback to pre-WWII municipal park district golf courses. It comes with Outta-Gah-Mee Park on one side, which, aside from being a short 9-hole muni, is the major difference between Outta-Matic and, say, Triple-the-Pines, the jarring influx of civilization that comes with a public swimming pool down the left-hand side of the 1st hole. Then grassy park with barbecues south of that and a limestone pavilion, limestone bandshell, and a softball park encased in seating tiers made out of limestone further left. There is an area where people can board the riverboat replica The Carlsburg Belle that makes three trips a day up and down the Pentwater River and boards from a limestone dock. Conny was conjuring himself at 17 years old: 6'3" and 152 pounds, a tanned flank standing in the middle of the 1st fairway at Outta-Matic in the big hitters' landing zone having laced one off the elevated 1st tee, taking in the pool and the park, the river and the forest. Standing there with a cranium-massaging view of the area along the river being filled in by the 9 holes, including Outta-Matic's signature bantamweight 327-yd. par-4 3rd hole with its island green formed out of a natural inlet in the Pentwater. The pump house that supplies water for the course is still located along the river on that hole, is still operational, and is made of limestone.

Conny thought about his choices on the morning of July 28, 2003, what would prove to be one of the most beautiful days on record in Carlsburg, Keefe County, Chicagoland, IL. His drawer went in and out in phenomenal comfort.

"Let's call these guys" Conny said out loud, motored by puregrade concentration and a coital drive to perform.

The 3rd hole makes excellent use of a small ravine that creeps into the right side, ravines being somewhat rare for this area. And while it's probably more of a ditch per se, it's a strategically placed ditch. Pine trees lining the left side also add peril to the decision-making process on the tee, though they are a preferred peril to the ditch, past surveys have shown.

—*Chicago Golf*

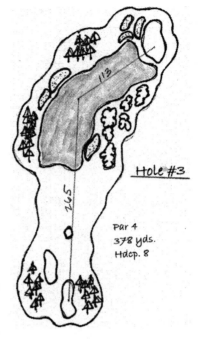

Hole #3

Par 4
378 yds.
Hdcp. 8

July 28, 2003 felt like the day Conny could finally break from the pack, establish himself as the best golfer of his close circle, best by far and most naturally gifted. He would play up to his true potential, and most importantly, never give an inch while in the heat of competition. It's only the golf course he plays against today. When he gets up on those guys he's staying up. Whatever carnage a 75 can produce, Conny will want even more because it's time to stop cutting these guys a break all the time. And hell with them if it hurts their feelings. "In fact, let's shoot for hurting their feelings" Conny said to himself audibly at his desk. Conny was a juggernaut then.

Buck was first to be called, as Conny's desire to besiege his best friend swelled mysteriously within him. The dialing was almost frantic.

"This is Bill O'Royerson."

"Hey Bucko."

"What's up, Bro?"

"9:34."

"No can do, Bro-mide."

"I don't have time for this, Buck. 9:34."

"You wouldn't believe how much work I got in front of me, Conny."

"You're right, I wouldn't."

"I'm serious."

"You're not *seriously* going to let this day go by without 18 holes."

"Well, I guess it's mainly about feeding my family and sheltering us all."

"Oh, you've seen them recently? How are they? The oldest one, is she still in high school?" Conny used a bit of a British accent for some reason.

"Hey, that's pretty good, Bro. Feeling pretty good, OK. It *must* be a nice day out."

"Have you stepped outside the tap yet this morning?"

"No."

"Do so."

"Seriously, Bro."

"Where's my Bucko, man?! B-U-C-K-O and Bucko was his name-o!"

"Holy shit."

"Come on, you ol' son of a bitch! I got you today!"

"Hi. Yeah, is Conny there, please?"

"Bucko!"

Conny was sort of floating on the effervescent aurae that ebbed and flowed from his cranium and watered his stamen. Meanwhile, Buck was trying to remember the last time he heard

Conny like this, and he was back at college and still searching the data banks laden with hops and barley not to mention kind bud and primo FUN-gus.

"OK, so you're going to take possibly the greatest day ever and use it to puss out, have I got that right? Wanna make sure my notes here are accurate."

"We get a day like this every July, Bro."

"My God. You're right. I'm sorry, Buck. What was I thinking. We do get one day a year like this. Here I am thinking they're like rare or something, but you're right, we get one *every* year. OK, well, seeya a week from Saturday then. Looking forward to broiling at 7:30 in the morning on the 3rd tee with you." Conny's sarcasm could sometimes be annoying.

"Who else you got, dillwad?"

"You know you're my first call, honey. You and me, Bucko. Who's money should we take today? Who are the unwitting victims of Force 2 From Namino, WI That Is?" (Buck and Conny had teamed up to win a 2-man better-ball tournament in Namino, WI a long time ago and apparently with great force.)

"Get Blurry and Simons."

"Any particular reason?"

"No particular reason whatsoever."

"What if I have to go with Not Worthy?"

"Then I'll not play."

"What if I said I want a Nassau?"

"What, you and me?"

"That's right."

"Ever hear of division among the team, Con-stance?"

"No, but I've heard of dissension among the ranks."

"Go screw."

"Hi. Yeah, could I speak to Bill O'Royerson, please? Yeah, the prematurely aging drunk who *used* to enjoy gambling? Thanks."

"You want a Nassau with me, Bro-mide?" It sounded like joy in Buck's voice.

"C'mon baby."

"You can get DeBerry and Sweet, II to fill out the foursome for all I care. You're on, you poor and apparently high bastard."

"Buck, I'm frightened."

"Just you wait and see."

That was it. Conny had peaked the addict. He could get Franklin DeBerry and Theresa Sweet to fill out the foursome and it truly would not matter. Buck was the other best golfer and the truest test Conny would find at Triple-the-Pines that day. Plus, it always fascinates Conny to watch Buck change under the pressure of competition in a seemingly endless array of twitches, yanks, and barks, and to realize that the only way he witnesses any sort of growth or signs of maturity in Buck is through the new ways he handles winning or losing. For example, one time last year, Buck was beating Blurry soundly in a Nassau during which Blurry would occasionally look at his cell phone like Sissy Spacek hoping to hypertelekinetically force it to ring with an emergency of any kind before entering the tee box of Buck's favorite 14th hole, but the phone eerily never rang for Blurry. Buck was up on the front-9 (he had won the front-9) and looking rock-solid on the back-9 and, hence, the total-18, the Old Style a miracle elixir that morning and the 14th hole looking to Buck like the home his faithful wife had kept up in the glen while he was away on the Crusades, it was that comfortable and reassuring. Buck parred the 14th, basically cinching the trifecta after a Blurry triple-bogey meltdown, and the phone still eerily never rang. So eerily, in fact, that Blurry rifled his glove compartment immediately upon walking off the 18th, battered, to make sure his records showed he made payment on last month's bill. As he stood next to his car, withered and sweaty, Buck said over to Blurry, "I certainly hope whatever damage has been done here can be restored by beer in the clubhouse, on me," which was in sharp contrast to a few years ago when Buck beat Pogo Foley and said "Take that, you little prick." This was how Conny witnessed growth in Buck.

Even though the mystery of wanting to damage his best friend lingered, dialing became free and easy.

"This is Tom Blair."

"This is Conny Bromenn."

"Con-sistently Bothered. Can't do it today, Conny."

"You gotta get real."

"Can't do it, Bro-dy."

"Can't or won't?"

"Never did know what that really meant, but pick one and it applies here."

"Come on, Blurry. You talk like you don't know how short life is."

"Made vastly shorter by my playing golf today, if you were to survey the wife."

"O'Royerson's in."

"Oh, well in that case I'll just tell Jennie hell with her and let's all get there as soon as we can. Play 36. Make a whole day out of it."

"Come on."

"Is he sober?"

"Do you *want* him to be?"

"Can't do it, Con-carne."

"If you don't play golf today, the void in your soul will grow even larger."

"At least there won't be a void in my wallet from getting robbed by *your* asses in a Scotch game plus whatever mind-fuck Oh,Drunkagain? dreams up."

"The winning attitude ladies and gentlemen, as taught by Vince Lombardi."

"You're the one that said I gotta get *real.*"

"Jesus, Blurry."

"Yeah. Who would I get stuck with?"

"Don't know yet."

"Not Worthy is not acceptable, you realize that, right?"

"Yep."

"What about Clark Bar?"

"Not sure if he's in town."

"It doesn't matter anyway, I can't do it."

"You will golf today, Tom Blair." Conny was in small-time carnie hypnotist mode. "You will meet up with good friends in wildly conducive golfing conditions, and play with them. You will imagine yourself winning at least for a good portion of the beautiful day."

"I'll have to imagine it."

"Mike Ditka, ladies and gentlemen."

"'*Cause I'm real …*" Blurry sang into the phone the tune of the Jennifer Lopez song, "I'm Real."

"9:34."

"*The way you walk, the way you move, the way you talk …'cause I'm real …*"

"9:34, dillwad."

"*The way you stare, the way you look, your style, your hair …'cause I'm real …*"

"Prepare for the worst. 9:34!"

"*The way you smile, the way you smell, it drives me wild …*"

"Oh, and remember to bring your cell phone."

"Oh, and remember to fuck off."

Only one more to go. Blurry being in was the next best thing to getting Buck because Conny, like Buck, wanted badly to corner Blurry's cell phone and melt that damn thing under the blue-flame intensity of a Scotch game, a Nassau, and maybe even one of Buck's bastardizations depending on how everybody felt on the 1st tee. Conny and Buck could formulate a game that would unhinge Blurry, pit several forces against Blurry all at once, those forces including the trappings inherent to the basic challenge of a game of golf and then adding a heaping of ways to gamble on said game, and combining that with Blurry's self-imposed Achilles' heel—the cell phone of course. Dialing continued.

"Hi. This is Clark Sweet, Midwest Regional Sales Manager with DuKeefe Mortgage. I'm not available to take your call right now, but please leave a detailed message and I'll get back to you as soon as possible. If this is an urgent matter, press the pound key now to reach Erin Cochran, Administrative Assistant. If this is an emergency, press zero to have me paged. If you are looking for Linda Hammond-Evans, she's no longer at this extension. Please re-dial the main number and ask for extension 24563. Have a great day, and thanks for calling DuKeefe Mortgage."

"Hi. This is Conny Bromenn from the Foundation for the Betterment of Conny Bromenn Through Golf. We have a charity golf outing we'd like you to participate in, pronto. Get your ass to Triple-the-Pines by 9:34. Call me. The day, she is glorious. Tell Erin I miss her, a lot, but that Linda Hamandeggs and I are very happy. I know Erin would appreciate that."

Getting only Clark Bar's answering machine did not diminish any of Conny's zing. He was needing an answer either way though, and soon. If Simons was unavailable and Sweet didn't call right back, going to Not Worthy could definitely bog Conny out a bit as far as zing was concerned.

"This is Bill Simons."

"Dude."

"Con-stantly Bothered. I was wondering if you were gonna get a game going. Saw the weather channel this morning. Can't believe it."

"9:34, man."

"Can't do it, Conny. I'm in Sarasota with the wife and in-laws."

The crackles of a cell phone any more than 20 miles outside its origins, much less from Chicagoland to FL, was unmistakable. Also, Simons had the ease in his voice that comes with telling the truth, which was very distinguishable in a guy like Simons, who often lied.

"How hot is it down there?"

"Can' t go into it right now. Must conserve energy."

"Pretty bad?"

"Well Bro, my ass crack is the coolest, shadiest place I know of right now."

"What's going on in Sarasota?"

"Debbie had flier miles to burn I guess and her folks wanted to see the kids."

"D-World?"

"Can you be parents with children and in-laws vacationing anywhere in Florida and get out of the state without going to D-World? They have D-Passports now that either get punched before exiting the state or I guess something like a cavity search ensues. You get deloused. We're going today."

"Sounds like fun in the incredibly unbearable sun."

"Mmm. Yeah. Bit of humidity too, you might say. I saw a poster for one of those rides that propels people from great heights down through water so that the splash is the thing, you know?"

"Yeah."

"Yeah. I'm gonna sign up for that one today I think."

"The power of the animal to adapt to his surroundings."

"Adapt or die, I've always said, Bro."

"Well, sorry to hear about your troubles."

"Who do you got so far?"

"Myself, Buck, and Blurry."

"My body actually like shook a little when I saw the weather up there. I want Triple-the-Pines so bad that I actually grabbed my crotch region."

"You always grab your crotch region, Bill."

"Yeah, but there was a somewhat apparent reason for it this time."

"Well, shake a bit in Water Mania for me."

"Alright. Play well."

"Always."

Though the beautiful air continued to waft over the window sill and affect his stamen pleasurably, Conny felt a bit stymied while he tested the drawer with the phone books as a slightly movable weight. Not Worthy? God, not today. A pause in the voltage. Then Conny's desk phone rang right in his face almost.

"Hello." Conny actually trembled.

"Bro-women."

"Clark Bars are Sweet." He then grew short of breath.

"Actually, they can get a little bitter when they beat your ass in golf."

Effervescence shot through Conny, maybe as never before.

"You're in?"

"Nah. Think I'll skip golf today, Bro."

"It's you, me, Buck, and Blurry." Conny thought about what it would be like for him to start crying on the phone with Sweet.

"Sounds great if those are the teams." Sweet almost outwardly admitted he's not a 7-handicapper, hoping to team with Conny for balance. But Conny knew he had him.

"Actually, handicapwise it works out better if it's me and Buck. But we can see what everybody thinks."

Sweet wasn't in a position to refuse that game, nor golf in general that day.

"That's cool." Sweet had sort of an ambiguous reply that said both it's cool if Conny and Buck are a team, but it would be cool to get a consensus on the 1st tee, but with an obligatory albeit minor emphasis on the part where it's cool if Conny and Buck are a team because why should it matter to a 7-handicapper, right?

"9:34."

"What are we playing?" Clark Bar had been so burned by Buck's incantations so many times, not to mention the more socially acceptable Scotch game and relentless Nassaus people inflicted in shameless exploitation of Sweet's ego.

"Not sure yet. Whatever we feel like. Scotch game probably."

"Doesn't even matter on a day like this." It mattered a little bit to Sweet.

"Working from home today, Clark Bar?"

"Yep."

It all fell together for Conny. He needed to remember he wasn't 17 years old just then.

"You wanna hit a few balls first?"

"Yeah, I can meet you at the range, Bro."

The forestation of Triple-the-Pines's north face creeps in from the right side, crowding this 4th hole. Golfers often find themselves taking more club as compensation for the possibly errant-right shot, as if a ball hit with a 4-iron is going to somehow miraculously burrow through overhanging oak limbs any more than one hit with a 6-iron would.

—*Chicago Golf*

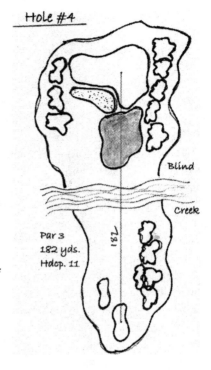

Hole #4

Blind

Creek

Par 3
182 yds.
Hdcp. 11

182

Triple-the-Pines is a public course greatly admired by the public and quite different from almost all Chicagoland golf courses these days in that, while it is certainly located within the boundaries of Chicagoland, it was not developed in conjunction with, or in and amongst, housing. This is miraculous because Triple-the-Pines is less than 25 years old. Even the most private courses built recently are unable to escape the bone-jarringly staggering development. Triple-the-Pines itself is surrounded by a few neighborhoods of Carlsburg, and not necessarily older neighborhoods, but it is not part of/central to the neighborhoods, much like streets or sidewalks or driveways or neighbors are parts of neighborhoods, which, if you play a golf course that was built in conjunction with a housing development, you might begin to feel that fairways are roadways or sidewalks and greens are places to be gawked at as if you were waiting for a bus. That isn't a feeling most golfers appreciate, or anyone appreciates for that matter, and certainly not what you go to the golf course to endure. These neighborhoods can't be seen from inside Triple-the-Pines's natural boundaries, which originally housed Hill's Best Pine Tree Farm, from which many of Triple-the-Pines's holes were carved, obviously. (When explaining the origins of Triple-the-Pines to guests and newcomers, guys have fun saying *Hill's Best apparently wasn't good enough* since the tree farm—where 50,000 white pines and other conifers and firs were planted in 1964—couldn't make a go of it, even though they were perfectly timed for the residential and commercial landscaping craze that would come with Chicagoland's population explosion's ravenous appetite for landscaping.) Triple-the-Pines's founders are highly commended on a twice-daily basis for their efforts to have found the parcel of Keefe County land in the late '70s and act on it quickly, creating the golf course with a wall of nature on its perimeter that secured Triple-the-Pines within it.

Though, there are other courses—lots of other courses—in Chicagoland that are very well built and fun enough to play and that have enjoyable clubhouses too. Guys explore them whenever the opportunity arises, oftentimes to see if they are as interesting as other guys have said, but also to compare them to Triple-the-Pines; to reassure themselves that they do actually have the incredible fortune to have wound up in a place where they can have more fun suffering a rain delay than they might have under the best weather conditions at any other course. True, Triple-the-Pines is their home course and as such it is indeed familial. Conny thought about many of the Triple-the-Pines family as he made the drive over. He thought:

There's Phil Black, who has been the greenskeeper at Triple-the-Pines since its conception and in the last 20 years has guided Triple-the-Pines to becoming one of the most beautiful *things* in Chicagoland. Floral and faunal magazines have had their covers adorned with Triple-the-Pines's flowerbeds, hedge patterns, and wetland species preservation efforts, for examples. County forest preserves call Phil for advice on how they too can make their forest look "so natural." Phil presides over a course that is highly sought after by golfers from all over, and has received merits for it by name in articles and via greenskeeping awards. Phil also has to deal with a "domestic situation" in his words, those situations often coming in the middle of the afternoon and sometimes in the morning, occasionally mid-day, and can prevent Phil from showing up at the golf course when he probably should sometimes. Which, because Triple-the-Pines's founders built a house as accommodations for the presiding greenskeeper not too far off the 12th green, the thought of Phil having to attend to a domestic situation all the time and never detailing what that situation might be, not that he has to, piques interest. Add to that the fact that he married Alana Ramirez, the collegiate beverage cart girl from a few summers ago. The rumor mill has produced actual grist that snows laden around the 12th green. Rumors seem to involve credit cards, phone bills, e-mails, a car that was repossessed about two and a half years ago, separate bank accounts, web sites, joint back accounts, spans of time spent apart, lack of time spent apart, her lack of a job, the free time it affords her and subsequent sub-rumors of things done behind his back during all this free time without his knowing about it via credit cards, phones, e-mails, and web sites, his insistence that she not have a job so that she rarely leave the 12th green area, ever, her interrupted college career, much mutual resentment, their age difference, in-laws, and sex. It's interesting how rumors about Phil and Alana can reflect the mood of a foursome. For example, if: It's Fri. afternoon and work has gone well that week and guys were able to put together a game on the spot without interference (wives), then: Phil Black isn't supervising the development of that new sand trap out on the 16th hole like he should be because of it's in lieu of some afternoon delight with that saucy 25 year-old Mexican wife of his, and who the fuck could blame him, come on, have you seen her in that sundress? However, if: It's Sat. morning after an almost job-threatening work week and getting "clearance from the tower" (wives) to play that morning proved particularly challenging for guys, like let's say there was actual yelling involved, then: Phil can't get through to Alana from the clubhouse phone to see if she wants to meet for lunch, his treat, because the bitch is probably on-line looking for illicit anonymous fuck partners, come on, have you seen her in that sundress?

And there's Theresa Sweet, who is Clark Bar's 16-year old niece known as Sweet, II. She manages the range, selling tokens for the range ball vending machine, making sure it stays full, collecting empty buckets, and operating the range ball retriever, which is a small tractor just bigger than a riding lawn mower. The tractor has a protective cabin obviously to deflect incoming range balls, and the range manager prior to Sweet, II, who was Ethan Wagner, customized it. Ethan apparently altered the range rover by sneaking onto the range on his last night of summer before going back to school and reinforcing the already-enforced cabin of the tractor by draping an awkward chunk of chain-link fence over it, which, it would be found out later during fall, was not so adeptly clipped the chunk of chain-link fence wasn't from the back-end border fence of the range. Ethan then apparently employed some bungee cords, again maybe not so adeptly, and painted "Le Cage Afoul" in quotes on both sides and the front and back of the rover with a surprising and undeniable flair for calligraphy. To be honest, Sweet, II was initially disappointed by the sight of "Le Cage Afoul" on her first day (Sweet, II's), but as she began to find out that a lot of guys had a penchant for making games of aiming for "Le Cage Afoul" while practicing on the range, Ethan's added armor proved to be just the security blanket Sweet, II needed in order to collect the range 4 times a day, 6 times on Saturdays and Sundays. Luckily for Theresa, "Le Cage Afoul" has taken on a personality that guys like, and so talks of repairing Ethan's repairs have quieted for the time being. Good news, because that extra layer of chain-link fence has become tantamount to her being able to just get in the damn thing anymore.

And Marti Lynn Morley has been the beverage cart crew lead gal for five years now as most of the other girls work it as a summer job in college while Marti Lynn is 37. She takes palpable joy at usually being the only woman on the entire golf course, and with all the beer. Her smile is broad and sincere and it fits her entire body perfectly. She has lovely bright and brownish hair that O'Royerson secretly views as a light indicating that it is the beverage cart when the cart is too far away to tell for sure and he's very drunk, much like the light atop a police squad car in the night. Marti Lynn has the body of a 37-year old woman who does not work out and is slim in some places but not others, like her obliques and breasts. Other than skin softness and hair quotient, her body doesn't really differentiate too much from a lot of guys except for the breasts, though they certainly offer Triple-the-Pines an appreciated piquancy on a slow weekday or drunken weekend. Marti Lynn has been divorced twice, just coming off a divorce after 16 months of marriage to Jeff Habberson, a mortgage broker from Cook County who has golfed many times at Triple-the-Pines but is not a member (passholder). Habberson apparently mistook Marti Lynn's enjoyment of being the center of attention among hundreds of golfers across 120 acres—mixed with the fun of operating a beverage cart, roving the entire plot, and displaying her entire being upon pulling up to each foursome, her generosity of spirit that is and whatever summer clothing she can get away with at Triple-the-Pines—for meaning she was probably a swinger, which, turns out she isn't. This proved to be a long-term bolstering of Marti Lynn in the eyes of most guys but a major short-term buzzkill for Jeff Habberson. And Pogo Foley epitomizes the mid-20s-years-old assistant pros that seem to dominate the assistant pro circuit. He's in his mid-20s, lean and diminutive, a long-ball hitter whose major challenges to getting to the next level are, aside from the emotional capacity needed to be a winner, putting and ball striking. ("Ball striking" is a term for how cleanly or purely someone can strike the ball, especially with their irons, and one of the many terms in golf that can seem excruciatingly redundant [of course you have to *strike* the ball] but has somehow entrenched itself in the vernacular, another good example being when someone hits a nice shot, it's not uncommon at all for other players to say "helluva *golf* shot!" or sometimes just "*golf* shot!" The most ridiculous of these, though, has to be "So-and-so really knows how to *golf his ball.*" This term, *golf his ball,* is used in all seriousness by golfers, professional golfers, and golf commentators, but many a listener has expressed doubt as to whethter *they* even know what it is they're really trying to say here.)

As Conny made his way across town, he thought about other guys, like Clay Schraeder, who is a 4-handicap with arguably the best swing at Triple-the-Pines and is so glaringly good looking that he seems to emit glitter over his skin and hair not induced by sweat. Marti Lynn Morley, on bad hair days, goes from a pleasant countenance to a stern visage when she's realized too late that she has pulled up to a foursome with Clay in it. Marti Lynn has been known to audibly curse herself after changing her countenance, and while *still serving* Clay's foursome's beverages. One time on an apparently particularly bad hair day for Marti Lynn, even Clay had to remark to his foursome about how she grumbled not so under her breath something about finally getting contact lenses after "Mr. Dickless pays the rent," which Clay suspected was Marti Lynn's way of expressing the trials and tribulations of alimony and how to collect it. Marti Lynn then speeding away bad hair flailing like a clump of golden reef-residing sea-life in the late morning sun, a beacon to O'Royerson two fairways over waving his white towel in one hand and Conny's white towel in the other quite desperately to flag her down, she was going so fast. It isn't the actual changing of her countenance that Marti Lynn seems to hate nearly as much as it is her *catching* of herself's changing countenance too late at the sight and hitherto unbeknownst personal proximity of Clay Schraeder, even though he does glimmer. Theresa Sweet has been seen running to make head-first fully extended body leaps into "Le Cage Afoul" as Clay Schraeder approaches the range, spending an hour (or however long it took Clay to complete practicing) collecting what was originally less than 20 balls across the entire range since she had collected the range 15 minutes prior to Clay's ascension. This is because Theresa finds the TTP uniform she has to wear somewhat unbecoming.

And Ken Blankenship is head pro at Triple-the-Pines and rarely plays golf and has never been seen swinging a club during lessons. Conny and Buck have played a few rounds with Ken but that was years ago now and even then, though able to score quite well, it (Ken's swing, game, general demeanor) wasn't ever what O'Royerson would refer to as "poetry in action." Triple-the-Pines being a public course, Ken isn't nearly as obligated to make nice with the golfers as much as a private club pro is. Sweet encountered hard evidence of this several years ago when he was invited to play Carlsburg C.C. for the first time, where he was astounded to see the head pro there, Samwell Forrester, come bounding out of the pro shop with a shining driver cradled under his arm and donning the whitest golf glove Clark Bar had ever seen, declaring to the general commotion that was the putting green that he was ready to employ the next installment of "what has to be the longest running, widest ranging, and most expensive golf lesson in history." Forrester then pulled a caddy up by his hair though the youngster had a red C.C.C. hat on over it, calling him "d'Artagnan," and telling him to transport his clubs "into the quiver that is my Sunday bag" and meet him at the 1st tee in four minutes, the sooner the punishment was administered, the better "for the local gentry to understand who remains their lord and king" Forrester explained loudly over the putters, some who were used to it and some who weren't.

And Franklin DeBerry is an absolutely horrible golfer; his swing not just devoid of any redeeming features but in fact quite troubled and a chiropractor's basis for all the reasons he/she goes into practice, not the least of which is the potential revenue generation—

particularly in repeat business—that could be experienced from the spinal abuse suffered at the hands of a DeBerryesque golf swing. Some guys call DeBerry a cross between Not Worthy and Arnold Palmer, if Not Worthy was horribly palsied and Palmer was dead. DeBerry can not break 120 if you pointed a gun to his head, a technique often fancied, but he will play 4 times a week during the summer and always with a good word for everybody, which guys figure is a testament, though not knowing quite what to, but the guys don't get the chance to employ their perception of what a testament is very much and so they sort of collectively perceive Frank as what they had always construed a testament to be, you know, somebody repeating something relentlessly even though there isn't a prayer of a payoff of any kind, which isn't necessarily a testament in and of itself unless it's *to* DeBerry's "great attitude" or *to* his "determination" or *to* his "blind fucking devotion." One time when chatting with guys after an early morning round, Frank related excitedly to them his par on the very difficult 15th hole and guys could just tell he wasn't lying and after getting out of earshot Blurry said "even a blind, rabid, disfigured squirrel finds a nut every now and then," which still doesn't technically complete the testament sentiment but guys figure *close enough*. As kind as DeBerry is, one of his kindest traits is to choose to play very early in the morning, before the pro shop has opened yet, alone most of the time so as not to inflict himself on other golfers that don't have unreasonable time constraints. Frank relishes the end of the 18 though, able to admit to himself deep down that the carnage of 120 is some pretty heavy duty, but he's still done by 9:00 AM, gotten a solid dose of early-morning Triple-the-Pines air, and guys are gathered around the putting green and in the clubhouse by that time and he can chat with them for a while over coffee without having inflicted himself on them, which keeps everybody at a certain level of ease.

And Clara Franta is one of the very few regular woman golfers at Triple-the-Pines and maybe the only one with a friendly wave and hello and downright discussion for guys on occasion, like she must have had older brothers or something, like somewhere along the line in her formative years she was made way more than just privy to the unique vulnerabilities and inabilities guys can face, and how often. So, when she sees guys she's able to laugh with them and *sub*jectify them, bringing into prominence each man's individuality while embracing the idea of men as a group to the point of them achieving "cute" for her, which of course makes her unbearably attractive to the guys, though she doesn't necessarily receive top-notch service from either Marti Lynn Morely or even the young Sweet, II. One time, O'Royerson, meaning to hit a few balls before a round, wound up next to Clara on the range, chatted with her overjoyously for about a half-hour while not exactly hitting balls, and promptly shot 102 that morning not for lack of practice so much as for hearing and seeing Clara in his downswing a lot. She has the banter and canter of a woman who was brought up by men but was lucky enough to inherit the eyes, skin, hands, hair, neck, and ass of a woman, and carries these aspects in a nonchalant way that men who are interested in women will fantasize about, but wonder if they would ever deserve. The list of those particular achievements of femaleness, by the way, was developed by guys during a self-challenge to make such a list while waiting on the 7th tee, the par-3 that can back up on Sat. mornings leaving two and three foursomes on the tee at the same time and inducing conversations about what are the truest indicators of womanliness, or, what turns you on most about women. The self-challenge was structured under the auspices that, if they had to spotlight the areas of a woman's body that are pillars of she-stuff without using the "majors," which were cited as tits, legs, feet, throat, and forearms, what would they be, but you *were* allowed to include the ass because guys just felt like they needed that consolation for some reason that morning on the 7th tee. Clara gets bandied about in conversation during rain delays sometimes as regards being competition for Marti Lynn Morley, legal competition anyway, since Sweet, II gets mentioned as well but under the kind of hushed tones that are so hushed they need to be accompanied by craned necks, eyes checking past points necks were originally craned for, and hands brought over mouths in a gesticulation smorgasbord, probably the only situation in which the guys could ever resemble, say, the townspeople from *The Scarlet Letter*. Clara winning for long-term companionship, but Marti Lynn getting the nod for the "short-term."

And Dr. Boskins seems to have been elderly even before Triple-the-Pines. Conny remembers him repairing a fractured leg when he was a freshman in high school Conny was and having stepped in a chuck-hole while caddying at Carlsburg C.C. and worrying whether this old doctor his mom took him to could handle the task. Boskins' general geriatric premise is based on his having looked like he was at least 70 for at least the last 20 years and is not just somewhat enhanced also by the fact that even though he plays three times a week, his golf bag is always somehow dusty.

And Edward "Apple" Hatch has possibly one reason to play golf four times a week at Triple-the-Pines during the fall and that is to see how many apples he can eat since they're free from small clumps of apple trees that grace the sides of a few of the holes, preserved by Triple-the-Pines's founders when building the course. So guys call him "Apple" and pretend to bite into an apple and cock their head and wink with approval of the pretend apple's tangy tastiness when they refer to him. Not too coincidentally, his cheeks are shiny and red Hatch's are, he weighs the same as when he was in the Navy, and he has absolutely no predilection for bullshitting around. Guys figure Hatch has an "apple-like" diet year round; he just likes getting them for free during the fall and does not "waste not nor want not" in doing so, it seems to Sweet.

And Claude Rebel always compares Triple-the-Pines to courses he plays in Florida during 2 months every winter, and comparisons are starting to repeat themselves at this point, which, they weren't super-appreciated the first time around.

Rick Hanson devotes Sunday evenings in the summer to playing 9 holes with his wife Cherie and is almost unrecognizable when doing so.

Carmine Bronsan whistles while standing over a lot of shots and almost right up until impact as a way of trying to appear carefree, thoroughly over-compensating to hide his fury at never breaking 90, but it's pretty transparent.

Tommy Sheehan knows how to twirl his club like a baton …

Locals commonly refer to the 5th and 6th holes collectively as "The Calm Before the Storm," not only because their conditions are relatively benign in comparison to the rest of Triple-the-Pines, but also because a lot of difficult conditions resurface after these holes, and in the form of *water*. Also, the 7th hole is officially named The Storm.

—*Chicago Golf*

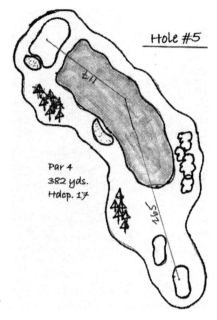

"Bro-mide!" Blurry brandished a bucket of range balls and a beer.

"Is this heaven no it's Triple-the-Pines." Conny did not pause in show of the routine of that line.

"Damn straight, Bro-dy."

"Grabbed a little energy bar for the range I see."

"How you gonna not?"

"Is Clark Bar here? He was planning to hit a few balls."

"The unmistakable silhouette of Clark Sweet does grace Triple-the-Pines's range's morning sky, each Sweet swing producing a graceful arc in said sky." Blurry pretended to look far off towards the horizon though the range was less than 10 yds. away from them.

"That's your first one, right?" Conny pointed to the beer.

"In my life?"

Conny was finding out that the beautiful day had not singled him out that morning. He was surprised. Guys rarely hit the range before a round, even at invitation and confirmed RSVP to do so; practice is boring and guys can be lazy, bottom line. But there Blurry was, and of his own volition. Conny turned to see Sweet on the range as well, and Blurry headed that way with nourishment and a smile. Conny was seeing in the competition both determination and joy at being on the range. Sweet looked focused, man. Conny realized then that, covered in aurae earlier that morning, he had been blind to the possibility that other guys could be experiencing their own personal smothering of aurae. Here they are *practicing* for fuck's sake.

"Clark Bar! Wow!" Conny approached the range with not mock praise as he was witnessing a nice mid-iron from Sweet, the ball starting low then rising as though propelled by a second booster-type engine. It was accompanied by the sound of a well-struck iron, which is the *cooshhh* of the blade pinching ball and turf simultaneously with immense impact. The thing about a well-struck mid-iron blade is that the sound so closely matches the feel, cushion-like when you've connected with the part of the clubface understatedly known as the "sweet spot." There is also a quality of echo.

"Con-stance."

"Where the hell did that come from?"

"I've been known to hit a decent 6-iron once in a while, Bro."

Man. Practicing *and* cocky. The day filled Conny's head, but as to cleanse it. The song "Rio" by Duran Duran overcame him, but was motivating.

"You're often the very embodiment of a 6-iron, Clarkie. I know that." Conny began to relish the idea of a good match.

Conny pulled two long irons from his bag and swung them, stretching, and bent in many directions from the waist, stretching more. Sweet used his 6-iron to pluck another ball from a pile near him and place it on a tuft of green grass that remained in a small brown radius where he had been clearing turf with each swing. He did this deftly, took another swing, and produced another fine shot, increasing the brown radius. Blurry slugged from his beer while leaning on his driver and watching Sweet's ball, then set it down and addressed a ball he had teed up.

"So how 'bout this day?" Blurry made solid contact.

"Unreal."

They had about thirty minutes until their tee time. Conny watched Clark Bar and Blurry limber up like a couple of mini-tour qualifiers except for one had a beer in his hand. Clark Bar continued to hit one beautiful 6-iron after another, the brown radius growing slowly rounder in a highly organized manner.

Buck O'Royerson is a person that seems to be at one with the world while driving his car. It's the kind of thing other people with cars envy. Buck doesn't have an overwhelming passion for cars by any means, and he mistreats his own 1986 Pontiac Parisienne in what seems like a series of attempts to see just how much the damn thing can actually take. But he drives at a pace and with a certain look on his face that is quite simply in tune with his surroundings, which seems to be a pace slower than other drivers around him, yet Buck never actually falls behind somehow. He gets passed a lot, but he never truly gets *behind*. He's the guy you passed 5 minutes ago but wound up next to at a stoplight five minutes later, Buck sipping over-contentedly from a coffee cup that didn't steam and finding the right song on the radio with a head-bob of approval, you pissed as hell that the light is red. The look on Buck's face while driving combines the following impressions: 1) Look, I'm driving, and 2) I can feel myself driving, and 3) I'm taking note of many of the things around me while I'm driving, and though I don't care too much about them I'm still happy they're there for the most part, and 4) I think driving maybe *is* a privilege, really. It's easy to watch Buck drive. When he pulls into Triple-the-Pines, the notoriety of his out-of-date vehicle and the way he drives it attracts viewers, friends mostly, and Buck pulling into Triple-the-Pines has a way of promoting cohesion among all its elements, Buck's Parisienne becoming a center that everything else groups around, a Pontiac nucleus.

"The torch has been lit!" Blurry yelled to Buck as he pulled into a parking spot.

"The marathoner has arrived!" Buck yelled back mutedly through his windshield though driver- and passenger-side windows were both down.

Buck was having a smothering of aurae for himself, and that set Conny's aurae ablaze, his stamen a jubilee, his brain a lightning-caused fire.

"Take a few swings, Bucko? Got some extra balls up here."

"Definitamundo."

Buck pulled his clubs from the back of the Parisienne and hoisted them on his shoulders with the routine that most people have to throw on a T-shirt. He walked slowly but with purpose straight over to where Conny was on the range, set his clubs down at an open space next to him, stooped to grab a glove out of a bag pocket, then stood up straight and smiled a catbird smile and took his time shaking each man's hand.

"Clark Bar. Practicing behind our backs?" Sweet had the fresh face of accomplishment.

"Blurry. A man after my own heart." Blurry held up his beer and nodded his head in a silent toast.

"Bro-mide. A man on a mission." Conny took stock of Buck. He thought that along with breaking 75, taking Buck in a Nassau was tops on the intrinsic fulfillment list that day and maybe the most desired byproduct of the beautiful day.

"How much time 'til we tee it up?"

"Got about 15 minutes. Nobody really out here yet though. No real rush." Conny was thinking about it.

Sweet had stepped back for a rest.

The range is irrefutably the key to healthy golf. It is the exercise and meditation before the challenge. It is the final reminder of fundamentals. Golfers know this, but what it takes for a lot of them to spend quality time on the range, especially prior to a round, is akin to what it takes to get the average person to go to the dentist. A lot of people do it. More people don't. But July 28, 2003 was different. The fact that all four men were on the range prior to the round says so. Emphatically. The beautiful day had a lot to do with it. See, in Chicagoland, when you have beleaguering humidity and heat or biting cold winds, or rain and mud, or rain mixed with snow, etc., it beats you down. It does not lift you up. It sure as hell takes practice out of the equation a lot of the time because who wants to stand out in that crap any more than necessary. In order to make up for that, in order to make up for the fact that a beautiful day may not arbitrarily smother them in motivational aurae, a lot of guys will engage in other forms of stimuli in attempts to achieve a zinging stamen. These attempts consist of: gambling games that have no relation to golf but are forced to fit into its arena anyway, too much beer and all that will ensue, chatter about work and wives and strip clubs and mortgages and car leases vs. car loans, chatter during backswings vindictively, vandalism, cart tipping is a favorite, penis flashing, fisticuffs, cart races, bumper carts, drunken cart races with beer can drive-by's then fisticuffs, and noises of bodily functions somehow held and timed perfectly to disrupt the most crucial point of the top of a backswing. So when a day like July 28, 2003 comes along, even though it seems like guys would be hopped up on zing and ready to step up their engagement of golf course theater warfare, the beautiful day actually has a reverse effect. Not just calming the guys, but supporting them so that they can then go out and really *try*. Apparently, since the day is already beautiful, guys don't feel compelled to manufacture their own beauty via cart tipping and penis flashing. On an arbitrarily beautiful day, they'll even practice. For the semi-regular foursome, a tremendously helpful side effect to being on the range together prior to a round is the time afforded to establish how they will gamble. Setting up the game on the range is ten-fold easier than setting it up on the 1st tee; there's simply more time. The gambling would probably be pretty basic on July 28, 2003, with more focus on shooting well and winning at straightforward competition. Conny, Buck, Blurry, and Sweet first realized this while hitting balls on the range at a point when two minutes went by without a single word from any of them.

Good drives on Holes 5 and 6 should give players a short iron if not a wedge into their respective greens, and the smart golfer will do what he can to take advantage of these scoring opportunities while he can. Some locals have actually muttered "and miles to go before I sleep" rather melodramatically upon walking off the 6th green, the level of melodrama coming in ratio to how poorly they may have scored here at the easiest juncture on the course.

— *Chicago Golf*

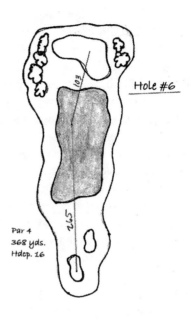

Hole #6

Par 4
368 yds.
Hdcp. 16

"So, what do we want to play today?" Nobody came forth. They definitely wanted to gamble, but in a wager that allowed them to *concentrate*. Something that forced them to think about golf, or else not doing so would have consequences. Actual consequences. Conny looked around and noticed that, although there was some activity at the clubhouse now, they were still the only ones on the range.

"Do we want to do a Scotch game today?" Ten beautiful 6-irons in a row had pumped Clark Bar up, to say the least.

A gambling idea had been tempering "Rio" in Conny's cranium since the minute Buck had pulled into the parking lot.

Conny felt like if he brought up his idea to the guys, it could possibly cost him his long-time friendships with them, and had the potential to worry Buck. No small feat. This idea could cast Conny in a different light, for life. All he knew was that he felt like he was waiting for something to happen and got the distinct impression that close to everybody else he knew was waiting too. Hell, people he didn't know looked to be waiting oftentimes. Many, many people looked anticipatory. His idea made Conny actually think of the word *unravel*.

A pause had materialized that forced the guys to move around a little bit, not uncomfortably but just frustratedly at not confirming a game and the tee time was closing in. Blurry went for his beer, Sweet took his glove off and shook it and put it back on staring at it anew as though it were a completely different glove, Buck switched from a wedge to a 7-iron and checked the two-pronged stand of his bag's frame for no reason since it was sturdy. Conny stood behind his range balls and glanced from the horizon down to the ground and back up.

Conny would have to do it before anyone else got to the range. He could see DeBerry mulling around the door of the clubhouse with coffee and in search of camaraderie. His idea was not ready to go past the current foursome.

"I've got a different kind of Nassau we could try." Conny coming up with a new experiment was pretty much unprecedented. As grumbles expectorated, Conny threw caution to the 275 yd. sign on the range with his driver. Somehow, just then, Buck, Blurry, and Sweet realized that Conny was going to be 40 years old very soon. Buck, Blurry, and Sweet could feel themselves remembering in unison that Conny had grown up absolutely loving golf, to the point that he tried to pace himself on his intake of the game, not play so much as to burn out on it, because he would've been heartbroken if he ever had to turn his back on the game and not because he didn't have the time for it, but because he just didn't feel like playing. They could feel themselves remembering that Conny was the editor of his high school newspaper. That he had gone to college to study journalism and English literature and still reads poetry if given some really, really spare time. That at 40, he was a real estate appraiser. Buck, Blurry, and Sweet felt this in unison, concurrently telepathically.

The sun warmed Conny's face unobtrusively, like a desired hand might, and he basked in it privately. He opened his eyes to see the guys in action, three human males who fit well into their clothes in spite of themselves and whom had chosen Triple-the-Pines as a haven from a much larger community of humans in an attempt to maintain decent mental balance.

Conny had garnered their attention.

"Instead of betting money on the Nassau, let's bet pacts."

What? Collectively.

"Pacts?" Collectively.

"Oh, Bro-mide."

"What am I gonna do Con-man, be your slave for a week if I lose? Mow your lawn? Do the dishes? Service the wife?"

They laughed genuinely.

"Come on, Conny."

"Pacts?" Collectively.

Stay with it.

"I'm totally serious. Let's bet pacts, like obligations."

"You really are high."

"Can I throw out an example to you, mon dillwads?"

"We're on the tee in like 3 minutes, Bromenn. Come on. Scotch game, $5-$5-$10 Nassau."

"One example?"

"It's alright, Buck. I gotta hear this."

Each man was facing Conny broadly and leaning on respective golf clubs, Blurry with beer in hand, too. Conny was over his range balls.

"Here's an example: Buck, if you lose to me, you have to run for city council."

There was an initial, split-second silence in which the four men changed aural direction in a way that mirrored slight wind in the treetops, their faces sort of re-molding to their stationary heads in a way that could not be mistaken for anything else but *sway*. Then they laughed partially genuinely. More like nervously.

Buck walked over and put the back of his hand to Conny's forehead, turned to the other guys and shrugged his shoulders. He put his arm around Conny's neck. "I see. And if I beat you, you weirdo, you're gonna run for city council?"

"No. I would have to initiate a car-pooling program for the Chicagoland area. Only it would be more like a law than a program. It would start out as a program until I could get a law made. I would consider a car-rationing arm to the program/law."

Quarter-second frozen silence. Partially genuine laughter. Notice taken that Conny is for real on this. Buck released the light headlock he had on Conny.

"Jesus, Conny."

"A car-pooling program."

"Can you make a law?"

"We don't have time for this."

"I'm dead serious about this." They could tell that he was. "You guys really wanna gamble? Let's *gamble*."

"OK, let me ask you this … What if we take on these so-called responsibilities, these pledges …"

"Pacts."

"Obligations. Agreements."

"They sound like contracts."

"What if we take them on, but in the end we fall short? What if O'Royerson can't get elected to city council because he's O'Royerson?"

"Go screw, Clark Bar." Buck swiped at a 7-iron with a nice little draw on it.

"What if I don't raise $10,000 like my contract says for the Little Sisters of the Blind? What if I raise $9,999.99? What if your blueprint for a car pooling and rationing program is met with the same reaction other car pooling and rationing program blueprints have already been met with, which is pretty much utter disdain, like 'fuck off if you think you're taking my car, my fucking car, away'?"

"Here's the thing: It won't be whether we actually meet the goal or not, it's that we have to genuinely try. If by the end of a year, we can tell that the guy is not really trying to reach the goal of the pact, the agreement, like if we take a vote and three of us unanimously agree that the dillwad isn't really trying, really trying, then he pays each man in the foursome $1500, pact ended." Conny was not afraid to show his enthusiasm at that point.

"You realize there are three bets per man in a Nassau, right Bro-mide? Front, back, and total-18? I'm assuming you haven't completely lost your mind here." Buck displayed intrigue unintentionally. "You realize that means that you would have to have like 36 pacts to cover the entire Nassau, right? A pact for if I beat you on the front, a pact for if I beat you on the back, and a pact for the total-18, a pact for if you beat me on the front, a pact for the back, and a pact for the total-18, a pact for if I beat Blurry, a pact for if Blurry beats me, for if I beat Sweet, for if Sweet beats me.... Do you have 36 pacts?"

"Yes."

"Bullshit."

Conny was walking up to one final range ball with his driver. "Who are the real gamblers here?"

Conny was over his ball at address, looking down on the ball, but he may as well have been looking each man in the eyes. He laced his driver in such a cannonade fashion that the ball had no flight "pattern." Just pure cannonade torque.

The Storm is in the far northwest corner of the golf course, where Illinois winds can sometimes blow a ball safely back onto land, away from 1831 Marsh's murky abyss (though apparently not quite "murky" or "abyss" enough to keep the average foursome from holding up play by searching for what they have to know are completely irretrievable golf balls).

—*Chicago Golf*

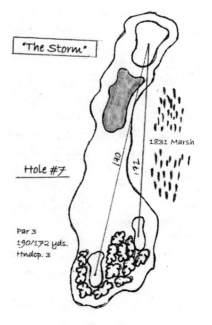

"What if we tie?" Blurry was unaware of the defibrillator his question was until he saw other faces expand with anticipation.

"Same as before. A tie negates the bet."

"So no carryovers?"

"How the hell are you gonna carry over a damned *pact*?" Buck's Irish may have been wearing thin.

"If you tied the front side, but lost the back side, the loser would have to uphold pacts for both sides. Get it, Oh,Drunkagain?. Someone, get him a beer. He's shaking."

"No. No carryovers." Conny was conscious of the sharpening questioning, the sharpening interest.

"Can you press?"

Buck turned his head away from the group and froze his body.

"Um, no presses."

"Blurry, how in the hell would you press a pact?" Buck spoke to the direction away from the guys, still frozen.

"Well, if your pact was to raise $10,000 for charity, if we tied the front I could press you on the back so that you'd have to raise $20,000 … Am I really the only one that sees opportunities for carryovers and presses in this game?"

"Not at all, Tom."

"I love that, actually."

"No presses."

"So what's to keep us from purposely tying each other?" Buck has actually done this before.

"Hopefully whatever shred of manhood you have left in that graying, wrinkled, and sadly never fully realized sack of yours."

Pogo Foley stuck his head outside and yelled at them. "You're up!" The sun was mirrored in the high-gloss paint that surrounded the doorways and windows and it made Pogo brilliant too. He thumbed towards the 1st tee, his voice and gesture said he tired of having to do this every time, though it hadn't become crowded yet that morning and guys rarely needed to be called to the 1st tee from the practice range, of all places.

As they began to make their way over to the 1st tee, they met with Janice Canby who was coming up to the range, and who had the unbecoming habit of saying "Look at you" and then adding an action, "Look at you (*action*)," which is two-fold unbecoming particularly for Janice because 1) it's a collegiate colloquialism, a habit that probably originated on campus a number of years ago now and with a collegiate-level exaggeration on the "you" reserved specifically for college students to say things like "Look at *you* studyin'" or "Look at *you* orderin' pizza" or "Look at *you* watchin' Soul Train" but Janice is 41, and 2) even for college kids that's getting to be pretty rote by now. Janice said "Look at *you* guys goin' to the 1st tee." She managed to embarrass them. The break in conversation that being called to the 1st tee and being embarrassed by/for Janice Canby can cause is about as solid an interruption as you can get, aside from someone involved in the conversation actually walking away, and Conny wondered how he would keep his idea for the strange Nassau alive. They started walking again.

"Of course, 36 pacts won't be awarded, so to speak. Everyone would have to lose everything for that to happen. Somebody's gotta win. Plus there's always ties." Conny softened the numbers and mentioned winning.

"But there is potential for a guy to have to uphold nine pacts, right? If he lost to each man on the front, back, and 18?"

"Yes."

"That seems kind of heavy-duty. I mean, I don't want to wind up having to create a scholarship program for autistic kids, organize sandbag routines for idiots that live in flood plains of the Mississippi River, and run for mayor of Carlsburg next week, and still have six other pacts to fulfill by the end of the year."

"I'm just saying, you wanna *gamble*? Let's make it mean something. Let's face consequences in losing. Let's almost load our pants at double-bogey."

"Well, there's no way you can communicate 36 pacts to us before we tee it up and I'm not going into a bet where I don't know what the damn pact is." Guys mumbled in agreement with Sweet. One of them said "communicate" again.

"What if I gave you a few more examples as a cross-section of what you can expect, knowing that I have 36 of these at the ready?"

They were passing Triple-the-Pines's modest clubhouse with its high-gloss details on their way to the 1st tee, the clubhouse flushing out July with open windows and air conditioners turned off. Pogo overheard "cross-section" and "36 at the ready" outside the window as he reviewed the starter sheet and sighed like his life was on the line.

"OK, let's hear it."

Conny continued: "Other examples include establishing a scholarship program for community college-directed students. Instead of asking the average 17-year old to recognize and declare his path in life one year before graduating from high school, this scholarship would somehow emphasize the indecisive nature, on average, of the first two years of college. Funds—which could be minimal since it's for a local ju-co—would be awarded based on the best essay on 'How the First Two Years of College, on Average, Merely Represent My Turning 18-19 Years Old' or something like that."

"You know, if we don't allow O'Royerson to establish Nassau values anymore, what does it say if we decide to go with this?"

"I agree with Clark Bar."

"I know more than a few parents who might back that ju-co scholarship thing though."

"Aren't there already some ju-co scholarships?"

"Yes."

The perfect temperature delighted them. Conny felt like he could climb a tree, no problem.

"Another one could be initiating Domes for Co-Dependents, or D-CODE, a program that builds refugium for people who are disparagingly co-dependent on addicts." Conny wasn't going to give up.

"Domes."

Somebody said "refugium" again.

"A place where they can go hide away for an hour or a day or a week and they don't have to 'join' or follow or whatever. They can just hide."

"Domes of Enablement."

"If they want to *join* something later, fine. Each refuge will be dome-shaped because co-dependents are often looped on something too, just to handle it all, and domes are easy to recognize even when fucked up and in crisis. Non-addicts who depend on co-dependents are welcome too, since dealing with co-dependents can be just as frustrating as dealing with the addict, on the whole."

"Co-co-dependents?"

"Would a co-co-dependent want to huddle in a dome crammed with co-dependents? That sounds like their worst nightmare."

"Maybe they each get their own room."

"If you're looking to hide, wouldn't the domes kind of give you away?"

"These are the details you'll be asked to iron out."

"You're out of your freaking mind."

"Buck's right."

"Another one could be to write, then market, an article series on the subject of how turning Amish could be more exciting and rewarding and logical than space travel ever could be, as far as truly constructive learning-adventures go, not to mention way more cost efficient, with the cost savings going back into preserving where we know we *can* live. Like instead of spending $4 billion dollars to find out that the moon and Mars are dead, we could've had hydrogen fuel cell technology implemented in cars *and* homes by this time, avoiding pollution and war on Earth, where we do live. That type of thing."

"Amishnauts?"

"Does one 'turn' Amish?"

"I say the money we've pumped into space exploration over the past 40 years could've gone towards developing the hydrogen fuel cell that whole time. We could be 100% energy source self-reliant by now, with just the money spent on finding out that the moon and Mars are dead. Why wouldn't we do that?"

"You haven't really thought this out, have you?"

"Another would be to initiate a back-to-basics program called Physio-'Neers that replicates living life according to how the pioneers did with regards to diet, exercise, and conservation, i.e., how those things just naturally evolved around the way they had to live life back then. Physio-'Neers would emphasize that maybe the pioneers didn't have it easy but maybe they had it right, and marketing materials for the program would come with a logo of a fit, modern man wearing overalls and pitchforking symbols of modern waste, like pitchforking an oil spill or a TV or something."

"Did you know that we're real estate appraisers?"

"I'm in regional sales for mortgages."

"Physio-'Neers."

"Didn't I see that on PBS?"

"Well, sort of. Except I'm not saying to throw out all the modern conveniences, nor am I saying dress like a pilgrim."

"So, basically, your answer is organic farming. Become an organic farmer."

"I can see that. One could be to take recycling to the next obvious step by forming a grass roots movement that advocates restricting humans to only consuming—and by that I mean digesting as well as, you know, *buying*—only the most immediately biodegradable materials possible, hence, eliminating a recycling concern. This could be a possible arm to 'Physio-'Neers.' It seems like it might have potential to provide more copy too if needed for 'Amish vs. Outer Space.' It's fuzzy, but I think there's a correlation there."

"It's been so long since I formed a grass roots movement, though."

They approached the first tee, pressing against the slight hill that it sat on until reaching the mostly level tee box and finding where the blue tees were positioned that day. Conny, Buck, Blurry, and Sweet each set their bags down to kick out their stands, the plastic bottoms of bags not absorbing the force very well and shuffling golf clubs noisily. The four bags dropping, shuffling, and kicking out sounding like a short lit string of once wet but now dried firecrackers. Each man drew a breath and admired Triple-the-Pines and the horizon and the sky of the beautiful day in congress. *I'm not so sure, Conny ...* ran concurrently telepathically. More than one crane swooped and landed over by 1831 Marsh, the vast wetland that borders Triple-the-Pines to the west and comes into play on several holes. The wetland's name signifies the year that Carlsburg was founded and also signifies that everything else had been named after early settler Col. Erasmus Ambrose Bettinger so much that people were sick of it (Bettinger St., Bettinger Park, Erasmus Ambrose Bettinger Elementary School, Bettinger Memorial United Methodist Church, Bettinger Woods, Col. E. Ambrose Bettinger Community Center, Bettinger Memorial Congregational United Church of Christ, etc.) and so they named the marsh 1831 Marsh, even though Bettinger was responsible for conducting the most state-of-the-art geological surveys of the day and preventing other settlers from trying to build part of the town there, which would have surely sunk. When cranes swooped and landed on 1831 Marsh, nothing became unsettled when they did so.

While not the most severely angled dog-leg by Triple-the-Pines's standards, which is like saying a tree isn't very tall by the Redwood Forest's standards, still, if one does not make it to the corner with their drive here, their approach shot may as well be hit *from* the Redwood Forest given its chances for reaching the green.
—*Chicago Golf*

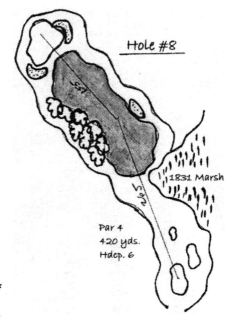

Hole #8

1831 Marsh

Par 4
420 yds.
Hdcp. 6

Each man grabbed longish clubs, held them out from themselves and turned at their waists. Sweet engaged in a dramatic stretching of his hamstrings that involved his trying to touch his nose to his kneecaps and he achieved a surprising amount of success at doing so. Buck swung two long-irons together. Blurry hoisted his driver over his head then behind his shoulders and continued to twist. Conny looked the men over and calculated their interest level while he readjusted the folds in a scorecard.

"10–12 pacts would probably cover it." Buck was revealing.

"You're considering this?" Sweet looked up from his right knee.

"What'd you expect?" Blurry was dispensing his empty beer can. "If you had a severe gambling addiction and someone raised the stakes to even higher than money it*self*, what would you do?"

Buck tried to ignore Blurry. "Let's vote right now if we're going to do this. But we need to know the exact bets or pacts or whatever for the front-9 before we hit our approach shots here on the 1st hole. That's twelve possible pacts, Bro. Can you give us that?"

"A mental spreadsheet, if you will." Blurry chortled, remained carefree, and noticed that Marti Lynn Morley was gleefully loading up her cart on the side of the clubhouse. You simply won't find someone happier in her work than Marti Lynn at the point that she's loading up the beverage cart. Buck looked over and thought Marti Lynn's hair was like a small fire above her head, and he was thankful for its alert. Marti Lynn looked up at the perfect sky and calculated it in terms of how influential it could be on a person's desire to drink.

"Anybody want one?" Blurry jogged over to Marti Lynn. Each man agreed to an initial beer, Blurry's buying being too much of an incentive.

"If I start now, I can have the front-9 spreadsheeted before we hit our approaches here on 1."

"We would have until then to decide?"

"Yeah."

"And it has to be unanimous?"

"I suppose it would work like any other Nassau. Those who want in—that is, those of us who are not named Mary Ann—are in. Those who don't and are, aren't."

"You present a spreadsheet, then we decide. And if we vote 'no' do we go with the usual $5-$5-$10?"

"I suppose so. But I'll have 12 pacts before our approach shots here. If you guys eventually find your gonads and vote 'yes' like gamblers would, I'll have the back-9's 12 pacts ready by the time we head for the 10th tee, with the final 12 pacts for the total-18 to be explained over the last 9 holes."

"I hate that last part, Bro."

"Yeah, way too much leeway for improvisation there, Constance."

"Pacts have to be set before play. Everybody knows that."

"I agree with Buck."

Conny's zing had actual texture.

"OK. Fair enough. I'll have pacts for the back-9 on the table before we even hit the turn, then the remaining 12 pacts to cover the total-18 before teeing it up on the 10th. But if you guys vote 'yes' to my initial 12 pacts before our approach shots here on the 1st hole, almost as if you were men, then you have to accept my next 24. There's no room for debate or pact swapping."

One of the guys said "pact swapping, yes."

"You better start laying it out, then." Buck had bagged his two irons, selected driver, grabbed a tee from his pocket, and tossed it in the air. It pointed toward himself. He threw it up again, pointing in the direction of Blurry as he walked up to the tee box from Marti Lynn's vocation. He threw it up again and it pointed toward Sweet. "OK, the batting order to start out with is me, Blurry, Sweet, then Conny."

"What about the Scotch game?" They had been sidetracked by all this talk of pacts.

"Scotch game teams should probably be me and Conny. What's your handicap these days, Clark Bar?" Buck sneered over at Conny because Sweet could never look anyone in the eye while telling them his handicap.

Conny started bringing forth pacts for the front-9. "Buck: If I lose to you, I have to initiate car pooling/rationing legislation. If you lose to me, you have to run for city council. If you lose to Blurry, you have to start on D-CODE. If Blurry loses to you, Blurry has to start on Physio-'Neers. If you lose to Sweet, you have to build the ju-co scholarship foundation and choose the winning essay. If Sweet loses to you, Sweet has to research humans consuming/buying only immediately biodegradable materials."

"*Let's get Physio, Physio. I wanna get Physio. Let's get into Physio …*" Blurry began to sing to the Olivia Newton-John song, "Physical." "*Let me hear your body talk, your body talk …*" He goosed Sweet with a 3-wood while singing.

"I'm serious about this now. You have to live up to these pacts if you lose or you pay out $1500 a man. I mean, that is the bet." Conny hated to quell any building enthusiasm.

"What's the bet on the Scotch game?"

"Dollar a point?"

Eyebrows raised a little, then total agreement.

"Three presses a side?"

"Wait a minute." Buck absolutely loved to press and hated limits.

"Buck, there's no way I'm taking a fifth press from you guys on the last hole not knowing what kind of pact I'll be stuck with too. No way."

"Clark Bar's right."

"Alright. Three presses a side."

Buck was teeing his ball up, his amphibious-looking torso more limber than it looked like it should be and looking like it could pounce, but amphibiously; his round stomach and bowed out fatty legs somehow got out of the way of Buck's mind. Buck had never been thin before, but he was always athletic and he was able to do many things with an athletic attractiveness. Backing off the ball to get a view from behind and swinging his driver to reacquaint himself with the weight of it, he pictured the idea of flying Blind Creek, a 232-yd. carry to do so that morning. Buck indicated telepathically that he would probably take on Conny's Nassau, and that he was going to be tough about it. "Here we go," Buck thought he was saying internally but was actually audible.

Buck's tee shot on 1: As Buck addressed his ball with mellow waggle, Conny realized that Buck *had* been sober on the phone that morning and that he may not have gone out last night; that he certainly didn't sleep in the parking lot, which was not uncommon. But a lot can happen in an hour between a man and an Irish coffee, especially when that Irish coffee is more Irish than coffee, and exponentially so when it's just Irish in a week-old White Hen coffee cup. Buck was loose from the range, from a little morning Irish, and Marti Lynn Morley had been sighted early, which was comforting. Buck breathed in deeply, put his ball off his left-foot mid-toe region in alignment (Buck liked a little extra room compared to the traditional ball off the left heel with driver), locked his gaze on the ball so tightly he could be reading its label, then took the one-piece swing Buck takes when sober, the club brought back on an inside path until it reaches the top of the backswing at precisely 90 degrees parallel to the ground, then brought back through on the same plane on the downswing, right elbow tucked, head perfectly still, Buck's semi-bloated body ignoring its fat and remembering its muscle. Buck's wrist action at impact smacks like a slapshot, and considerable torque ensues due to his excellent timing, hips turning properly this time, lots of leg drive, leg drive an indicator of Buck's early training back in the 70s and very important to his torque. On this drive, Buck's body was well balanced with a complete follow-through. It's a very functional swing, very fundamental (aside from a tailored alignment), but something about Buck gives it a panache it might not experience in other hands. His ball was a low-riser that flew Blind Creek by about 15 yds. and would eventually leave Buck about 178 yds. into the green.

"Beauty."

"Golf shot, Bucko."

"Blurry: If I lose to you, I write and market Amish vs. Outer Space." Conny was riding the crest of Buck's excellent start.

"Good luck with that."

"If you lose to me, you have to volunteer with the Northern Pentwater Valley Chapter of Habitat for Humanity to make it possible for a low-income family to get an affordable house by offering an interest-free mortgage."

"You're nuts."

"You would offer financial expertise. The house is also made affordable by community volunteer labor force and donated building materials. You would volunteer time for labor. Also, it would have to be a Blitz Build."

"Dare I even ask …"

Buck and Sweet and Blurry frothed a bit in their own aurae, absorbing the sun and reflecting it too. Blurry had already taken 3-wood from his bag, not wanting to risk trying to carry Blind Creek, not that he had a prayer of doing so, but Blurry sometimes liked to make a little show of having to decide whether he should go with driver on The Noose or lay up in front of Blind Creek, not that he's ever once tried it with driver. Blurry teed his ball up then stood behind it for a view of the hole, checking his grip as though he were working on something new each and every time.

"Blurry, if you lose to Sweet, because allowing humans to consume only the most immediately biodegradable materials possible is most likely a way's off, you would have to cooperate with current recycling efforts by initiating a program that puts what people intend to recycle to better use in an attempt to control and possibly reverse the amount of land being used for land-fills."

"Recycling the recycling." Blurry took some fluid practice swings.

"Your program would help people find local charities to donate the materials to, or organize group sales with the profits going to charity."

"It's got garage sale written all over it."

"Massive, massive yard sale."

"Or maybe even create a cottage craft industry based on people's recyclables, percentage going to charity."

"Yeah, count me in on this, definitely. I've always wanted to create a cottage crafts industry. And out of other people's shit. Don't know how I got caught up in the real estate appraiser thing."

"Didn't I see an article in the *Chronicle* about somebody trying to do this?"

"Yes."

It was 9:40 and they were still on the tee. Pogo Foley peeked out the window and winced.

"If Sweet loses to you Blurry, he has to develop a common sense parenting program for parents claiming to have troubled elementary or high school kids. It would not assume that their claims are unfounded by any means, but it would ask them to test the best of the child-rearing techniques of parents who reared the WWII generation."

Blurry was close to comfort with his grip, looking at the hole ahead from behind his ball.

"The program could hinge entirely on the near-total elimination of television, to be substituted by outdoor activity, gainful employment, and what would seem by today's standards to be almost abusive sacrifice-making. To the point that if a child wanted something, from a music CD, or should I say iPod, to having their own phone line installed, or should I say cell phone, they'd actually have to earn the money to pay for it."

"You're lost."

"It would be something parents can at least try before hiring the local pharmacist. Again, if you lose to Buck, Physio-'Neers, if he loses to you, D-CODE."

Blurry addressed his ball, still with a carefree glow that almost made him look like someone else. Blurry was the right weight for his height, technically, but he had a very round stomach the size of a perfect half-basketball, brought into stark relief by Blurry's very narrow shoulder region, thin legs, and a head that would've been too small for any of the hats in Triple-the-Pines's pro shop. Guys would never say Tom looked unhealthy, or even uncomfortable, but there was something out of balance there and it started with a half-basketball for a stomach. Most notable in Blurry's appearance that day, however, was a lack of cell phone on his belt.

Blurry's tee shot on 1: With one last check for grip and alignment, Blurry took the two-piece swing that will never allow him to be a single-digit handicapper, taking the club back from the outside then hitching at the top of his backswing to redirect the club to God willing the proper inside plane, hopefully finding the slot, but losing considerable torque and control in the process because he's Blurry. Tom's self-professed affinity for major two-piecers Lee Trevino and Fred Couples is his downfall via his attempts to emulate them. On this drive, a devotion to follow-through takes a ball that he caught a little off the hozel (the area where the clubhead is fastened to the shaft, and one of golf's areas in its bottomless pit of sexual innuendo) and keeps it on a straight albeit knuckle-balled path down the fairway, probably 25 yds. short of Blind Creek. It would leave Blurry with about 225 yds. to the green, an approach shot he is well familiar with here at The Noose.

"That'll work."

"Sweet, If I lose to you, I have to organize a proactive campaign to keep The Masters tournament commercial-free on CBS. I would begin by organizing and marketing an article series and possibly even a book. It's downright eerie how little that broadcast has been hailed for its efforts. I mean really eerie. Good lord, even golf magazines themselves … where are they on this? In this day and age? The fact that The Masters is broadcast today on TV without commercial interruption should lord over everything else in the game, if not everything else on TV, maybe everything else period. I mean, it should go like:

'Well, Lanny Wadkins, it looks like Tiger Woods is going to win his third Memorial Tournament here today.'

'That's right Jim Nantz, and that means there's 45 weeks until we see the next commercial-free broadcast of The Masters.'

'Right you are, Lanny.'

Commercial-free anything is shocking, but The *Masters*, on *CBS*, during the Tiger *Woods* era? It's nothing short of a miracle. I mean, I wanna meet tournament director Hootie Johnson and really get to know him. Hell, buy him dinner. He brought TV back to a place its inventors had originally imagined. Plus the fact that golf broadcasts are by far the worst offenders of commercial interruption than any other form of television today."

"Are you starting you're campaign now, with us?"

"You think golf has more commercials than a movie on TBS?"

"Definitely. I've timed it. I think that 1) golf broadcasts do go to commercial more frequently than anything else on TV, ABC's broadcast of the British Open possibly the most disgustingly jarring and regrettable example of this, every other golf broadcast on ABC running a close second but don't get me going on USA's broadcasts, commercial sieves that they are too, and 2) this is made all the more deplorable by the fact that, until the last group is on the last hole, golf *has* no interruption. There's no 'time out.' Somewhere someone is playing golf, and they're close enough to the lead to merit watching. Golf broadcasters want so much for viewers to believe in the unpredictability of the game of golf, but then they only follow like three guys the whole way, going to commercial between every shot almost. When those three guys are in between shots, show us the other guys that are a stroke or three off the lead. They're fun to watch too, is what I'm saying."

"More than *movies* on USA?"

"Or movies on TNT?"

"Or morning television, anywhere?"

"What about ESPN? They're awful."

"Or the last four minutes of a basketball game? You did say any 'form.'"

"Blurry's right."

"Really any sportscast at any time anymore. TV time-outs? Are you fucking joking? I was once watching liposuction surgery on TLC and when they showed all the fat from this giant chick's abdomen, my first thought was of all the TV time-outs during football and basketball."

"I shit you not, I timed the British Open."

"Or movies on AMC?"

"Or Bravo?"

"You know who's not too bad? BET."

"I timed the British Open during the final round last year when Ernie Els won in that playoff. I timed it from 9:22 a.m. to 10:45 a.m. CST on Sunday. Pretty much the primest time of the tourney. During that span of approximately 83 minutes, and this is the honest to God truth, there were about 32 minutes of commercials, and I'm not including minutes where they do those pop-up commercials for ABC programming at the bottom of the screen, which by the way how annoying is that. You know, 9:33.35 to 9:39.18 would be golf, then 9:39.18 to 9:42.10 would be commercials. This is during a major. The oldest tournament there is. At that time, there had to be at least 10 guys who had a legitimate shot at winning. When Els hit that famous bunker shot, we didn't get to see it live because they were away at commercials. Els is making miracles happen out of coffin bunkers, but we're watching commercials for erectile dysfunction. It's literally absurd."

"Comedy Central's bad."

"The Lifetime channel scares the he*lllllll* out of me."

"Telemundo never seems that bad, though."

"The Oxygen channel. Ouch."

"Yeah, Sweet's right."

"ESPN2 must signify two-times the amount of commercials, is my guess."

Sweet was teeing it up, and had also chosen 3-wood, which was a bona fide decision-making process as opposed to Blurry's little production because Sweet could sometimes carry Blind Creek if well oiled (either naturally or via substances). That was not his approach to The Noose today though.

"Is Conny getting off light here? Buck has to run for city council or create shelters for co-co-dependents, Blurry has to figure out the recycling problem in relation to the Earth's population explosion, I have to create better parents, for fuck's sake, but you *write* about the Amish and the Masters?"

"It actually sounds pretty even to me, Clark Bar. I wouldn't want to have to write all that, man. Plus car-pooling legislation? Right … Plus that Amish vs. Outer Space thing would be a *series*, right Bro?" Blurry was pumped by being in the middle of the fairway, first drive.

"Sweet, if you lose to me, you have to save Girl Scout Island."

"Sorry?"

"Girl Scout Island is suffering from erosion, but it can be saved by planting certain water plants along its shoreline. You would have to work with the Carlsburg Park District, organizing the fund-raiser necessary to buy the plants and recruit volunteers to help with plantings, you being the first recruit."

"Right. Got it."

Sweet was standing behind his ball and lining up the 1st hole. He took some practice swings, each one stopping half-way in the backswing so that Sweet could remind himself to keep his right elbow tucked, which Sweet considers, not erroneously, to be imperative to keeping the club on the same plane, back and through.

"Again, if you lose to Buck, you research humans consuming and buying only immediately biodegradable materials. If Buck loses to you, ju-co scholarship foundation. If you lose to Blurry, common sense parenting program based on WWII generation. If Blurry loses to you, recycling the recycling program."

Sweet is broad in the sense that his body is wide but not in the sense that it is powerful. There is a great distance between the two ends of his shoulders, though they are not strong nor does Sweet himself seem to be aware of their breadth. Sweet's taller than the average bear, which brings even more into stark relief his powerlessness. Sweet also has the swollen gut of a 40-year old desk occupant who hasn't given up Italian beef sandwiches and onion rings just yet, but there are also "patches" of his stomach that show through his shirt; uneven little mounds. Things attached to the surface of his stomach, it seems. There is no symmetry to Sweet's legs; they don't look like they should go with the same body. If you were given headless portraits of Sweet, one from the front and one from the side, you would never guess they were of the same person. Weirdest part of all? Sweet has a perfect male buttocks. The perfection of Sweet's ass is undeniable, and it lives in a spotlight especially given the imperfections of the rest of Sweet. Sweet's ass looks like it was sculpted with the idea in mind of exaggerating what a perfect male ass would be. It is so perfect that heterosexual men discuss it openly and so objectively that "attractiveness" is never a consideration. Really. It's just a *thing*. Buck has said Sweet should be an "ass" model. A body double, but just for the ass. Guys have agreed.

Sweet's tee shot on 1: Sweet's fundamental set-up is integral to his success as a golfer, as he mysteriously cannot generate the cannonade torque Buck and Conny generate, mysterious when given the breadth of Sweet and some secret ass-perfecting gene. The reason for Sweet's non-torque issues is hidden to the naked eye, as is the intrigue of golf that will keep certain personality types coming back to the game—to solve mysteries. Sweet looks like he's generating considerable torque, but only medium-range torque ensues as indicated by somewhat lifeless 250-yd. drives (especially for a 7-handicapper, right?). But his address to the ball tends to keep him on the straight and narrow, if not long. He took the 3-wood back fluidly on that first drive, the fluid swing allowed by his proper stance, maintained excellent balance as it was fresh in his head from the range (balance not just coming to Sweet, but has to be remembered), and turned on the ball with excellent timing in his hip-turn, his lumpy hips hanging over his waistline in dichotomy to that ass. Conny always suspected a lack of leg drive for the lack of power. Buck always suspected and would voice that it was a lack of manhood. On this drive, an all-around solid swing produced a nice drive for Clark Bar, his ball landing left of center in the fairway and rolling to within about 10 yds. of Blind Creek. He would be left with about 210 yds. for his approach shot into The Noose.

"OK, Clarkie."

"You're safe there I think."

Conny pulled driver from his bag, lightheaded from zing.

"And to reiterate: If I lose to Buck, car pooling legislation. If Buck loses to me, city council campaign."

"Absolutely crazy."

"If I lose to Blurry, I write and market Amish vs. Outer Space. If he loses to me, Northern Pentwater Valley Chapter of Habitat for Humanity financier and laborer."

"It goes against everything I've worked towards."

"If I lose to Sweet, I help Hootie Johnson maintain a commercial-free Masters tournament on CBS. If Sweet loses to me, he saves Girl Scout Island."

"Wake up, Bro-mide."

"Oh, I think my alarm just went off, motherfucker."

Conny's tee shot on 1: As Conny addressed the ball on the 1st tee that day, his body appeared to have *extra*. Conny appeared to be larger, as though he were outlined and then fleshed out to the very edge of his new outline. He brought his club back smoothly, strongly, his left arm a steel beam swiveling. His head did not waver, nor did his eye from the ball. He brought the club down through in a way that deceptively looked to have the same speed as his backswing. A free-flowing yet guided downswing produced the crack of titanium that would impress any golfer, cannonade torque having ensued. The ball did not catch up to what just happened to it until it was flying Blind Creek. Conny's ball flew to Buck's ball then rolled another 10-15 yds. He was dead center of the fairway, with about 165 yds. left for his approach. "Rio" blared.

While the tee shot here at The Duck Blind is certainly one of the most generous at Triple-the-Pines, the second shot into this 553-yd. par-5 is laden with various kinds of trouble spots. Oddly enough, it has been said that being familiar with the 9th hole's subterfuge is not necessarily an advantage, thinking psychologically.
—*Chicago Golf*

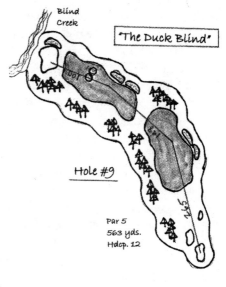

Straps of bags came to rest on their shoulders, and as they walked the guys began to discuss the mechanics of the swings they just took and the results. People were pulling into Triple-the-Pines's parking lot. Doc Boskins pulled his bag attached to its pull cart out from his dusty trunk and golf pencils settled around it when he let it land on the ground. Sweet, II walked from her car to the modest clubhouse with the slightly ruffled look that said she had been called in outside of her scheduled hours to accommodate the beautiful day. She tried to commiserate with Marti Lynn Morely about it but instead received a pat on the shoulder and a point upwards towards the sky and then beverage cart. Roland Messacar stood at his open trunk and had his pants unbuttoned, completely unzipped, and down around mid-thigh, butterflying his legs out in order to keep them there while he tucked his shirt in, his shirt being very long and Roland liking it as tucked as tucked can get. No one has mentioned the men's bathroom as possibly a better alternative for a place to tuck his shirt in so meticulously, though someone probably would if Roland were ever to stick around for a couple of beers, i.e., Roland then becoming relaxed enough to discuss the subject and guys becoming relaxed enough to bring it up. That opportunity hasn't presented itself yet. Clay Schraeder emerged from his new silver Mercedes and he outshined it. Phil Black rode a fairway mower as quickly as the giant mower would go and in a perfectly straight line (impossible as that seems over a golf course) that Phil has obviously practiced many times from the 1st fairway in the direction of his 12th greenside home. Phil controllably leaned forward in the seat of the mower in an attempt to see if that would make it go faster. Ken Blankenship was nowhere to be found.

"You in or out?!" Conny called over from the middle of the bridge as Blind Creek moved beneath him and Buck. Sweet and Blurry stood out in the fairway and waited for the other to answer, to the point that they had sized up their shot, made club selections, and stood at their ball to see if they were comfortable with their approach shots.

"Don't puss out." Buck had all but told Conny he was contractually in. Now he hoped in low tones that the other two would not puss out.

"What happens again if I lose to O'Royerson?"

"Christ in a plaid pair of pants! He already went over all that!"

"Physio-'Neers!" Blind Creek beneath them gave Buck and Conny the impression that they needed to yell more than they really needed to in order to be heard.

"Right, right. And what's that again?"

Buck gasped.

"You initiate a program where people can model their lifestyles, particularly as it relates to diet, exercise, waste, etc., on the Pioneers, taking a 'what's so wrong with going with things that we *know* work as opposed to flailing away blindly *all* the time in the name of progress' type of approach!"

"Like, American Pioneers, right?"

"Is he kidding, Bro." Buck then gasped again.

"That's right!"

"Those are just the ones we know about." Sweet was debating the potential of the pact wager with Blurry out of earshot, which was seemingly easy enough to do since Force 2 From Namino, WI That Is felt they had to yell from the bridge. "Who knows what this burned-out headcase intends to inflict on us for the back-9 and total-18."

"What could it hurt?"

"Say that six months from now when Audrey Hepburn Bromenn over there has you delivering Unicef to Pakistan."

Blurry turned to the bridge. "Would we ever have to leave the country?"

"What?!"

Buck did the frozen look-away, a bit of a sight on the bridge over Blind Creek.

"Each pact will be performed right here in Pentwater Valley!"

"I don't know. I feel good Clark Bar."

"Say that six months from now when Brother Teresa there has you knee-deep in the Pentwater planting water lilies around Girl Scout Island."

"That one's yours."

"Exactly."

"I'm in!" Blurry yelled to Force 2 then stood behind his ball and measured a line through The Noose. Conny and Buck did jigs on the bridge. Sweet slumped.

"$1500, Blurry." Sweet tried to dissuade his teammate.

"I don't think so, man."

Blurry's approach on 1: Going with 3-wood, Blurry caught it squarely and the ball took a straight line with purpose and came to rest about 10 yds. short and left of the green.

"Not bad, Tom!"

"It's up to you, Clark Bar!"

"$5-$5-$10?" Sweet was testing Conny to live up to his word of a normal Nassau being an option.

"Would you please grow a cock!" Buck was testing Sweet, in general.

"Who knows, Clarkie. You might not lose." Blurry felt good about not topping his approach shot into Blind Creek, or hooking/slicing it into the woods, or putting it in a sand trap. He had hit his 3-wood over 200 yds. and relatively straight. He would be chipping and from not too bad a spot. Might even catch a decent lie.

"What's $1500, right?"

"It's a lot to each of us."

"Alright, I'm in."

"You gotta live up to it, Clark Bar!" Force 2 yelled.

"I said I was in, didn't I."

Sweet's approach on 1: Sweet had chosen a new-fangled "rescue" club from his bag, a supposed substitute for a 2- or 3-iron, and caught all of it in a nice-looking low riser but pushed it a bit right, eventually landing in The Noose's right greenside sand trap. Sweet never knows what will happen to his bunker shots, but he caught his new-fangled club well, which was positive.

Given how much acreage the fairways of Triple-the-Pines take up, surprisingly little amounts of time are spent standing in the middle of one, much less purposely so from a tee shot, so when it happens, guys will sometimes try to carpe momentum as much as possible. Buck did so by pretending not to know exactly which club he would use for an approach shot that he must have hit a thousand times before. He finally took a 6-iron from his bag unaware of how much he was emulating the pros and their processes and procedures when selecting club in the fairway and sizing up a shot. *Good lord, one time in the fairway and he thinks he's Nick Faldo*, ran concurrently telepathically via the guys. Buck signified that he was officially in on the Nassau.

"I guess the worse that can happen is Carlsburg gets a man on city council." (This wasn't necessarily just bravado. Carlsburg's city council was considered to be made up completely of women, even though Nate Cash had been councilman for the 4th Ward for almost 16 years, but something about his having run uncontested in the lethargic ward for each term made him so less of a "man" to some of the guys that he was considered to be essentially the opposite of a man, which guys figure even in today's climate is still a "woman." This assessment of Nate comes off seeming particularly unfair when knowing that some of the guys *live* in the 4th Ward. Aside from Nate Cash though, the rest of the council was indeed comprised of women, as was Carlsburg's mayor. She was a woman, too, it had finally been decided after much debate by guys over beer in the clubhouse.)

Buck's approach on 1: Choosing 6-iron, finally, from 178 yds., Buck hit it decently though a tad fat ("fat" is taking too much turf). But more importantly it was hit straight, landing just short of the green but right in front of it where there is a thin strip of fairway-length grass.

The next 13 yds. between where Buck's ball had been and where Conny's ball lied were like a weight instead of distance. The din of pacts in Conny's mind; the hammers of Habitat for Humanity; heated city council meetings concerning zoning coming after heated disputed controversial campaigns for city council; the tone of Amish articles to be written and the outrage at casting outer space out as a human option; Pentwater River splashing over goulashes and water lilies; "Rio;" it was all sucked out of Conny's head, as was his zing subsequently. The guys following Conny to his ball and then huddling around him swept them all into a pile next to Conny, and their motion sucked everything out of him. Conny had no way of being sure about what a vacuum felt like, but he figured this had to be it. He could actually feel the flow of his blood changing. He really had Buck and Blurry and Sweet in. They were *in*.

Conny's approach on 1: From 163 yds., Conny picked out 8-iron from his bag with a little less flare than Buck's previous presentation. He swung it a couple times. Conny got over his ball with extra. He made excellent contact from a well-balanced swing, but a sometimes problematic strong grip turns the club-head over too much and pulls the ball left a bit, pin-high, left fringe/rough, ball not exactly sitting up. Conny wouldn't know what kind of lie he had until he got there.

Getting "up and down" means hitting a chip shot from not too far off the green or from a bunker then making the ensuing putt. It gets mentioned in the same sentence oftentimes with a "save" and indicates that the player did not reach the green in regulation. *He got up and down to save par.* The ability to get up and down is widely considered to be the pivotal skill in golf and the one that makes the difference. To scoring, to everything. (Golf's canon of sexual innuendo certainly does not suffer from it either, of course.) This skill is probably most crucial to the weekend golfer. As long as he can project the ball a good distance off the tee, the once-a-week golfer with decent ability would be smart to practice chipping and putting almost exclusively since he will not have time to perfect an iron-game, ever, and even if he did, he still has to *putt*. It may not be as exciting as hitting drivers and 5-irons for an hour, what is, but somewhere along the line a weekender either becomes more excited by a 79 with six one-putts than an 85 with a bunch of great drives, or he doesn't and accepts losing a lot. Buck has referred to this discretion as "the epitome of the old tortoise-and-hare syndrome," even though speed is not at all an issue here, but patience does linger around it somewhat so guys figure *close enough* and have never called Buck out for an explanation. Professional golfers have days where they've hit 10 out of 18 greens in regulation and can still shoot par or better by getting up and down. The weekender, even the solid single-digit handicapper, will not hit even that many greens in regulation and will be spending most of his strokes trying to get up and down from 5-20 yds. off the green, bottom line, fact of life. Witness these guys on the 1st hole:

The hole had actually turned out to be closer to the front edge of the green than its red "position" flag indicated. (At Triple-the-Pines, there is a small red flag below the larger yellow flag and it can be moved up and down the pin to help players out in the fairway measure the depth of the hole on the green. So, if the small red flag is high on the pin, that means the pin is at the back of the green, then the further down the pole the red flag is, the closer to the front of the green. Positioning of holes [and, subsequently, red flags] is up to the discretion of Phil Black. Red flags not corresponding to pin placements exactly is a common malady that Phil takes full responsibility for, and *with pure glee* guys often conclude. "Red flags indicate the *area*" Phil has to say. "Back *area*; middle *area*; front *area*" he will reiterate without anger or exasperation in his voice, and in fact with genuine interest. "How are we supposed to know *exactly*" guys ask. "Well, let's see," Phil will say, "you've got sprinklerheads all over each fairway with laser-technology measured yardages on them telling you to the inch what the distance is to the middle of the green, other markers in the fairway at 200, 150, and 100 yds., mature red maples to the side of fairways as 150-yd. markers, yardage books that are the result of laser-technology measuring available in the pro shop, and red flags to show you whether the pin is front, back, or middle. If you take a cart, you have a GPS system [global positioning system, seriously] installed on your cart to give you pinpoint accuracy, much as I fought that one. After that, I suppose actual *feel* would have to enter in somewhere." Phil is somehow able to take more interest in this thrice-weekly discussion as time goes on. He never tires of it, and while he discusses it at length from a chair at the unorganized wooden tables in Triple-the-Pines's modest clubhouse, coffee that is always tepid and rusty from Triple-the-Pines's deteriorating coffeemaker will steam from Phil's cup and appear rich-tasting to him. Oftentimes, mallards entrained in a blue sky can be framed in a window behind him, an enthralled Phil at the forefront with healthy color in his face.) On July 28, 2003, the red position flag on the 1st hole seemed to indicate that the pin was maybe middle-back. In fact, it was middle-front, a difference of almost 10 yds. Given how clear the atmosphere was that beautiful day, once the guys were up at the green, they were pretty sure the red flag was not being completely honest with golfers.

Blurry was furthest away, about 20 yds. short-left of the green, so he would be first to chip on. His optimism at having not gone in a bunker quickly faded when he saw how deeply covered his ball was by penal rough. Not Worthy would have claimed he needed to pick the ball up in order to truly identify it as his. The guys wouldn't exactly put it past Blurry either, probably because they might not put it past themselves, so they all watched as Blurry surmised his shot.

"Can't even tell if this is mine." Blurry chuckled and secretly hoped one of the guys would suggest moving it to find out for sure.

"Pretty sure that's it." Buck had ambled back from his ball a little closer to Blurry so as not to be in Blurry's path and so as to make damn sure Blurry didn't move the ball.

Blurry's chip on 1: Opening the clubface of a 60-degree lob-wedge that he has no idea how to use correctly, Blurry took really a feeble swing since there was no way for him to know what was underneath his ball. Stopping his swing at the ball and looking up early in desperation hoping to see a ball pop out nicely from the depths, the ball in turn never had a chance and lurched like a white round toad in thick grass, about 6 in., max.

"Damn it." Blurry was still away.

Blurry's second chip on 1: A little more sure of what's underneath now, Blurry applied a more commanding stroke, the ball flying forcefully out of the stuff this time, landing about 3 ft. past the pin and, with absolutely no action on the ball, the knuckleballer rolled another 15 ft. It didn't look great but deep down Blurry was just happy to be on the green.

Buck's chip on 1: Though Buck was in the fairway, his shot was still quite a poser as the pin didn't offer much room to stop a ball on the green. As a gambling addict, Buck can't refuse himself attempts at pro-level craftsmanship, so he decided to hood (close the face of, or de-loft) his wedge and hit it into the rise in front of the green in hopes that the ball would then decelerate and nestle cozily to the pin. There's lots of uncertainty in how a ball will behave on such an attempt and even for the pros it's usually a somewhat desperate option used in much more severe conditions than what Buck was facing here. Buck pulled off the first half of the shot gracefully. However, the ball and slight rise in front of him did not cooperate well with each other and the ball fell short of Buck's cozy hopes, barely reaching the green and some 12 ft. short of the pin.

"Hit that just like I wanted to."

"Could that have been the problem?" Conny had no problem chastising his partner when he took really stupid shots.

Sweet's bunker shot on 1: The ball was sitting up very nicely, and in the hands of pros this shot could go in the hole with amazing frequency. But to the weekender, sand is a frighteningly unknown quantity where the success rate at getting out is akin to winning $50 in the Little Lotto when stopping for gas. Sweet did all the right things, opening his stance and the blade of his sandwedge, taking the club back and bringing it through a little more quickly than on grass perhaps and with strong acceleration, letting the bottom of the wedge do the work to bounce the ball out. He also did all this while hitting almost 3 in. behind the ball, which in this case is about 2 in. too many. But the ball wobbled out of the trap and about 2 ft. onto the green, and even though he had about a 25-ft. putt, at least he was out of the damn trap. The guys were actually relieved for Clark Bar, as something about his not getting out of a bunker on the first try could've let a little air out of the whole foursome. Golf has a strong empathetic nature that way a lot of the time.

Conny's chip shot on 1: Being only about 3 ft. off the green, maybe 18 ft. from the pin and ball sitting up fairly well, Conny took dead aim on the hole, which was slightly downhill from him. He put a textbook stroke on it, short but decisive and devoted to getting *through* the ball—not hitting *at* it. His attempt looked and felt just like what they do on TV and the ball popped up and out about 4 ft. left of the spot Conny was aiming for and just sat there upon landing on the green, not even riding the downward slope more than a foot or two, never threatening the hole at all, leaving Conny with about a 10-ft. putt for par.

"What the hell?"

"That rough just ate your clubhead for lunch."

Now that they were all on the green, group aurae churned like cold surf to the concept of *score*. The guys were not mentally trained to take the game one shot at a time, one hole at a time, truly, though they had heard it mentioned on TV approximately 35 times a year for many, many years and claimed to follow it themselves. They began to start adding up what they thought would win the front-9, the back-9, and the total-18, all from what they had garnered after watching 3-4 shots on the 1st hole. Blurry was notably terse, being a stroke behind everyone else at that point. The man-hours involved in financing and building a Habitat for Humanity house clouded his vision while reading his putt. As did the term "Blitz Build."

Blurry's putt on 1: A 22-ft. putt that would reach a small crest about half-way on its way to the hole, it would then pick up a little speed on its slightly downhill path, breaking right to left app. 16 in. As he stood over his putt, Blurry was doing the math on an interest-free $170, 000 mortgage in comparison to a 7% $170,000 mortgage for a single mother who worked days doing light warehouse duty for a local manufacturing company while going to school at night to get her B.S. in Education and had three kids in grade school. He also pictured himself trying to use a hammer correctly. Blurry sighed, gathered himself, gauged his chosen line two or three times, caught a whiff of beer somehow, and stroked his putt with a final thought of *keep your head still*, a thought that didn't always come to Blurry over putts. His ensuing putt never hopped or wavered, looked like it was actually *hugging* the green's surface, rode the break circumspectly, and did find the hole with such precision that the ball clapped the plastic bottom of the cup and sent out the unmistakable muffled little echo indicative of putting perfection. His entire round changed already, right there on the 1st hole. And, hell, he would be happy to volunteer for Habitat for Humanity should it actually have to come to that.

"Great putt, Tom!"

"Workin' man's bogey, to say the least."

Now, guys who are app. 15 ft. away are hoping just to two-putt to tie Blurry, and the only thing on Sweet's mind at about 21 ft. away is *not* three-putting, which isn't the greatest frame of mind to have going into a putt of any length, especially for a 7-handicapper, right? Blurry went from being a stroke behind to setting the bar. The putter is universally known as the "money stick," and Tom Blair had just given an example as to why, magnified. Sweet congratulated Blurry again, sincerely, and sized up his own putt, the smell of Pentwater River knee-deep around Girl Scout Island very real to him, to the point that he looked around to see if a small stagnant pool of water had developed somewhere around the 1st green from recent rain.

Sweet's putt on 1: A long putt that would break even more severely right to left than Blurry's did, Sweet's thought standing over the putt was *try to get it within 2 ft.*, which was a lot of improvement over *just don't three-putt*. Sweet tried like hell to get the smell of old water out of his nose and started his putt out well to his right and did anguish until he saw the ball begin to break hard left towards the hole. However, the ball broke so hard left he soon realized it had no chance of reaching the hole and in fact began to curl back towards *him*, the break was so severe. The ball finally came to rest about 5 ft. away, but with a straight uphill putt left over. Sweet marked his ball.

Buck was hearing gavels as he lined up his putt and could not decide if gavels were still used in city council meetings to bring order, and would it really be necessary to try to *bring* order to a city council meeting? Probably.

Buck's putt on 1: Buck stood over his 16-footer very calmly, a beer in him now, feeling pretty optimistic about this relatively straight uphill putt. Sweet watched closely since Buck's ball would take the same line to the hole as Sweet's remaining 5-footer would. That is to say Sweet could learn or "go to school" on Buck's putt. With the sound of a pounding gavel that shook its base a bit, Buck stroked his putt. It was definitely tracking and a collective breath was held as the guys watched to see if par could be had on The Noose that day, but this was a brand of tracking putt that would not fall, turning just a little left in front of the cup as it lost some steam, catching some of its left edge and coming to rest less than a foot away. Buck tapped in.

"Your ass done got robbed."

"Great putt, Bucko."

Conny surveyed the break in his putt again.

Conny's putt on 1: He was in a good spot here, a 10-footer slightly downhill with about a six-inch break left to right, the kind of putt you feel like you can just send on its way and watch it make history. More importantly, Conny was a little anxious to get working on praising the efforts of the commercial-free Masters tournament, bring it into stark relief for our entire culture to see its colossus. Knowing that he would have to lose to Sweet in order to get the chance, Conny knew that such a highly desired reward for losing would surely carry him on to victory. In other words, Conny really couldn't lose. Dreaming of a beer with Hootie Johnson at Augusta National in Butler Cabin even though he wasn't sure if that's where the bar is at Augusta or not,

Conny stood over his putt and was intent but relaxed. As putter met ball, Conny could not resist watching the result, so much so that he may have peeked too soon, lifting his head just a touch at the crucial point of impact. As a result, the ball got pushed slightly to the right and without a very good roll on it, meandering hopelessly towards the general vicinity of the hole, finally winding up about 10 in. away. Conny tapped in.

"That was ugly."

"Buck's right."

"Less than mediocre there, Con-sistency."

Three bogeys were accounted for.

Sweet's second putt on 1: Clark Bar did go to school on Buck's putt, learning about the break-left just in front of the cup. Now it was just a matter of putting the right stroke on the ball. (An important difference to note between pros and weekenders on putts of this length is that pros don't even have a second thought about rolling a putt 3 ft. past the hole firmly. Well, they might have a second thought, but they replace it with a third thought that says something like *I'm a damn pro, for crying out loud*. Weekenders will try to get the ball to just fall into the cup, to just reach the cup, as opposed to giving it the kind of juice that could put it 3 ft. past because they *are* afraid of 3-footers, and with good reason.) Sweet stood over his putt and pictured three things: 1) people laughing at a 7-handicapper who double-bogeys a hole because he doesn't know how to hit out of a bunker and isn't a very good putter, 2) being on the first tee with the guys next time out and the look on Buck's face when he asks Sweet for his current handicap, and 3) 100 troubled teens and not an ounce of Ridlin in sight. Sweet put the tentative weekender stroke on the ball and it never threatened the cup.

"Up jumped the devil."

"Thank God for the 2nd hole, Clark Bar."

Scotch game: Force 2 From Namino, WI That Is went up 1 point (they got "total") on Sweet and Blurry. (No prox, no birdie, no low ball.)

Nassau: Conny, Buck, and Blurry were tied while Sweet went down one stroke to each of them. Sweet had no idea how water lilies prevent erosion, nor how to right the "parenting techniques in America" ship, nor what someone's used particle board credenza might go for in a recycling yard sale.

This is the first hole at Triple-the-Pines to bring large North Pond into play, oddly named because it is the only pond on the course and is located near its center. North Pond enters into the left side of the fairway and continues to border the green as well. Given the distinct possibility and subsequent psychosis of a poor score on the front-9, a shortish par-4 with water up the left side may not seem as simple as it sounds to start out the back side with.

—*Chicago Golf*

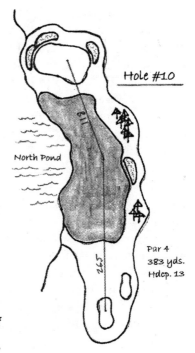

Hole #10

North Pond

Par 4
383 yds.
Hdcp. 13

265

The term "sweet spot" is a monumental understatement, and golfers need to find a more accurate way of describing the area on the face of a golf club that makes people ecstatic. True, it is difficult to express the particular vibe that comes from achieving 100% connection between the face of a golf club and a golf ball, that which sends said ball on the most highly desired path where it stays and then completes, all as the golfer had envisioned. Difficult to express the accomplishment, and the rapture. But "sweet spot"? Some golfers have offered "the g-spot" or "my o-zone" of course since the feeling is without a doubt akin to sexual climax: the unique build up prior to; taking your best shot at it, so to speak; feeling like an electrified pillar with limbs, for example, during; resting assured that you are capable of achieving anything else after. But it's still *different*. And while sexual congress might be close, "sweet" (would anyone want their top-shelf love slam to be described as "sweet"?) in almost no way conveys the overwhelming torrent of physical accomplishment and emotional fulfillment that a golfer will pose awash in as he holds his follow-through and gazes at his ball, realizing he has a well-struck ball in the air. *Attentive* understates, grossly, the golfer with a well-struck ball in the air. Maybe because the threat of it not happening is so absurdly abundant. That a clubface and ball can impact each other, with you at the helm, so as to render your body a small orchestra made up only of woodwinds as they find harmony is astonishing. A second, larger helping of astonishment comes when a ball can then be set afloat up in the sky after a breathtaking rise from its initial cannonade acceleration, there's that second booster propulsion, just look at it, then head either slightly left or slightly right depending on the spun action that is based on the golfer's individual swing, which is a mark of his individuality—the swing of the club and resulting flight path of the golf ball. These things cannot be replicated in any other way in the entire world. That's a natural fact. Even the good to great golfer never experiences the same well-struck ball twice. The perfectly launched golf ball is the stunning disclosure of revelation combined with the tangible proof of a bridge. Life becomes deeply enriched by having hit a golf ball perfectly. It swells inside the golfer to carry that experience in his heart for months and, inevitably, it brings him back to golf, sooner or later, with sooner probably winning out. The golfer needs to describe the part of the clubface that can do this as something far more than something "sweet." Even if the shot is achieved purely by accident.

Positioning your second shot here on the par-5 11th hole is key to ensuring a safe approach into its island green. Greenskeeper Phil Black has placed several traps at the end of the fairway in an attempt to intensify the second shot-making process. Turns out they only serve to make sure that players don't flirt with 1831 Marsh's danger in the very least, players laying up to what is a much better approach distance of about 100 yds., a real stroke-saver actually.

—*Chicago Golf*

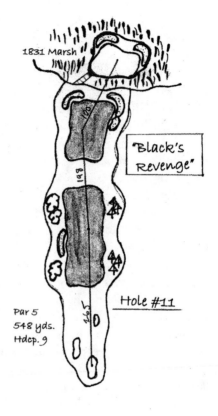

1831 Marsh

"Black's Revenge"

Hole #11

Par 5
548 yds.
Hdcp. 9

From the 2nd tee as it faces back towards the clubhouse, the foursome could see the practice green starting to swell with guys, many of them using cell phones to stave off the demands of their livelihoods and wives, keeping the world at bay from a practice green inside Triple-the-Pines. Craig Biitner wondered over the phone why it made a difference to Molly Biitner whether he spent his morning on the golf course or in his office at work. Either way, he was gone for the day, right? Clay Schraeder spoke softly and was very still except for a moving smile on his face as he stood there, shining, and efficiently pushed back morning meetings with several real estate appraisers. When his phone rings, Doc Boskins always seems surprised by it even though he has a thriving practice. He looks as though he's trying to find his cell phone on his belt even though it's always in the same place each time, then he will hold the phone up to his ear as though it is wet (the phone). A cell phone always manages to look small in his hand even though Doc is not a large man nor does he have particularly large hands. He has a way of crumpling a cell phone, though. The strangest part about it, according to Sweet, is that Doc's unfamiliarity with his cell phone doesn't seem to have anything to do with the fact that he's old, and "what does it say when a guy who might take out your appendix seems just naturally inept at finding and handling a cell phone that is always located in the same place, time after time." Marti Lynn Morley loaded up near the clubhouse and was happy to load and chat with guys who were on phones as they began to team, looking up and pointing at the sky and performing their version of *basking* while phoning. Pogo Foley emerged from the pro shop frenzied and pulling carts around while on his cell phone possibly with Ken Blankenship, who many times gives Pogo instructions for the day from somewhere else. Cam Phillips pulled a reversible lure from the zipper pin of one of the pockets of his overexposed golf bag, looked for a logical place to put it, smelled his bag while doing so, and was not on a cell phone.

Conny, Buck, Blurry, and Sweet accepted the 2nd hole's invitation, and started anew. After briefly summarizing the results of the 1st hole, each man managed to get off the tee to their fullest length, with only Buck ending up in the rough after he took the undisciplined swing that is not uncommon from the 2nd tee, the hole just looking so damn open and takable. Blurry again took 3-wood off the tee and hit an above average shot down the right-center of the fairway. By taking 3-wood off what is possibly the most open and accessible tee shot on the golf course, Blurry was making a bold statement that said at least two things: 1) he had formulated a strategy, and 2) he was using that strategy. A possible third arm to Blurry's statement was *I don't give a damn what you think about my strategy, I'm using it.* Conny's swing with driver was identical to his tee shot on the 1st hole. None of the guys could possibly be aware that Conny felt like he was 17 years old. He smoked it over everything and everybody to the left side of the fairway, which is the desirable spot on the 2nd hole for the big hitter as it gives chance to reaching this par-5's green in 2, the only par-5 at Triple-the-Pines to give guys such a chance. Sweet put double-bogey behind him and stepped up to the ball with the vigor he had been showing on the range, making it obvious to the guys that he was concentrating on remembering the range, and laced really a nice one down the identical path of Conny's ball except about 30 yds. short thereof. "Billie Jean" went off in Conny's head as they moved off the tee box into the fairway. He and Buck were out front of Blurry and Sweet as they walked off, and Buck disturbed Conny's groove.

"Hey Bro, why city council?"

"Maybe you could help in some areas."

"Like?"

"Monitoring municipal and construction stormwater permit applications, such as the wetlands and waterways dredge and fill permits."

"Oh, right."

"You could show a sincere commitment to the environment here on Earth, as oppsed to outer space, and help vote out those who promise the environment but really only like to see their picture on billboards every 4 years or so."

"Yep. I sure could."

"You could. You could influence zoning. You could make a motion to disband the current Planning and Zoning Board, en toto. Maybe Carlsburg doesn't have to become a mall, after all."

"Too late, Bro-mide. Anyway, why me?"

"The power is in the people."

"Um, why me?"

"Jesus, Buck."

"I'm serious."

"I guess I just think you could do it."

"But I don't want to do it. That is, I have no interest."

"Maybe if you start out feeling like you have to do it, *a la* losing in a Nassau, you might find it rewarding, deep down."

"City council?"

"You agreed to the bet, Bucko."

"Just curious."

Sweet and Blurry talked about mortgage rates and regional sales trips and strippers who looked like everyday women in a tone that said *down only 1 after The Noose to Force 2 From Namino, WI That Is; not bad.* This foursome was really out walking now. A wide open hole with nothing but Triple-the-Pines in front of them, and they pushed their strides and looked like 40-year-olds. Deep breaths were taken. Note was taken of the wind. The color green was overwhelming straight and down. The color blue was overwhelming straight and up. Blurry thought of the word *cooperation.* He thought he knew why but would hate to have to articulate it.

They began to fan out into different directions towards their drives. Buck and Blurry coupled up and began to walk together down the right side of the hole, the words "cell phone?" coming faintly from Buck and a response from Blurry that could not be heard, though a bounce in his step could be seen. Sweet and Conny started to take a path toward the middle of the fairway in the direction of their balls that were on the left side of it. They were getting into the shortened grass of the fairway. Sweet sidled up to Conny.

"Yo, Bro."

"Clark Bar."

"What about an article series on pros self-carrying their bags?"

"What?"

"An article series that proclaims the merits of a new rule in golf that makes pros carry their own bag." Sweet was speaking lowly and quickly, privately, but his voice still seemed to serpentine the pine trees that went down the left side of the 2nd hole.

"What?"

"Look, baseball hit the crapper a long time ago, and it didn't take football too long after that, am I right?"

"Yeah."

"Basketball has finally shit the bed, too."

"With ya on that."

"Much as I hate to admit it, golf is compiling some earmarks of the same type of thing."

"It's compiling earmarks?"

"It's got pre-decline earmarks, yes, but golf can be saved. Definitely. In fact, I think golf can either be on the cusp of failure or the cusp of supremity."

"Hmmh."

"It can look undisciplined and greedy and generally unattractive per basketball, et al, or it can keep its place as the unspoiled game. Maybe even be the one sport that takes a giant step towards challenging its players instead of grotesquely coddling them. I think self-carry could add centuries to the already centuries-old game."

"Gosh, Clark Bar. You want to write this series?"

"No, but I'm willing to take it on as a pact if I lost."

"Self-carry?"

"Those concerned about the direction 'technology' is taking the game of golf in should ignore the demolition of new equipment or the lengthening of courses as answers to keeping pros from continuing to humiliate some of the oldest greatest golf courses in the world and jeopardizing the game's integrity.

Those concerned should instead opt to campaign for 'self-carry.'"

"OK. You've thought about it."

"Professional golfers would have to carry their own bag. They have ridiculous new golf clubs and even more ridiculous new golf balls offering up booming drives and precision iron-play. All on perfectly manicured courses. Plus, putters of any length that can be *anchored* against/in any pit of the body a golfer so chooses. I grant you, the possibilities of the long putter could be vastly more interesting on the LPGA, nonetheless, I saw Kevin Barkin's kid Terrence lodging a long putter in his buck teeth in an attempt to completely eliminate wavering of the arms and hands, simply pulling the putter back as mandated by the length of putt then releasing the putter, and it swung like a perfectly working pendulum hung from the lad's erupting incisors."

"Did it work?"

"Come on. All of this is already so undignified that people either don't recognize the indignity anymore, or they do but they aren't willing to admit it, or they admit it but it falls on ears stuffed with money. And especially now with the kind of fitness regimens golfers are enduring—self-carry could make breaking 70 estimable again."

"Estimable."

"Breaking 75 might become notable."

"Yeah but Terrence is kind of a weird kid."

Conny and Sweet felt how comfortable the fairway was on their feet. The lack of wind and perfect temperature made everything seem effortless. Either of them could scale a pine tree handily in a lumberjack contest, they bet.

Sweet figures, if they enacted self-carry, professional golfers would never have to hear about the lack of endurance one can get by with to play the game. As false as that claim already is and usually from the thoroughly uninformed (though it can be hard to look at Craig Stadler, Sweet said, and justify golf's physical test, or John Daly, or Tim Herron, Kevin Stadler, Guy Boros,

Joey Sindelar, or Craig Parry; maybe a few others), pro golfers could really separate themselves from the athletic pack by taking on their own carrying duties.

"It's physical and *responsible*. See? We're talking about a major endurance test here."

Sweet thinks that it is amazing how blindly and how often the relatively capable and relatively smart weekend golfer who carries his own bag will wonder why he can't even contemplate playing like a pro while he watches as a pro never lifts a bag.

"They get to play in twosomes on manicured courses set aside only for them, while we labor in foursomes of 15-handicappers—maybe—on trampled courses and are asked to finish in *less* time than the professional twosome. High school kids play on football fields that are the same dimensions as the pros. Ditto basketball. Without getting into a whole big brouhaha about elitism here, do conditions for pros have to be *so* separate in golf though? I mean crazy-separate?"

Sweet knows the chasm between the pro and the weekender will always be vast, courses will always be different, time and devotion to the game and a natural gift for eye-hand coordination being involved and what not. Sweet thinks it's OK to give the pros certain advantages because "they deserve it just for devoting their entire life to the damn game, and nothing else" and as such they are an incredible thing to watch. But they need to be reigned in a bit right now, he thinks.

"I'm seeing cracks in the dikes, Bro-ham."

"I'm positive that you are."

Sweet doesn't know if watching pros carry their own bag would necessarily endear them to the golfing public. Hard to say. Would it diminish what a pro golfer is able to achieve with a caddy? Yes.

"And *there* would be professional golf's 'new' challenge. Are you telling me they wouldn't find a way to adapt to it?"

Sweet figures the USGA and Royal and Ancient Golf Club at St. Andrews (Scotland) are not willing to insert any other kind of challenge and in fact seem to be trying to sidestep any at all. Sweet notes Auggie Shopiere in the 2002 Greater Biloxi Invitational smoothing away sand behind his ball in a "waste bunker" while on the 18th hole in a playoff against poor Ned Briara who really got duped on this one, Shopiere getting the OK to do so from Delta Tour officials even after hundreds of calls came in during the telecast from avid golfers who assumed there just had to be something wrong with that. *The guy is smoothing the sand away from directly behind the ball* and *he's literally lifting the ball from its original lie* and *would he like a hoe for that?* being some of the reactions. Apparently, sand in a "waste" bunker is considered loose impediments somehow different from sand in regular bunkers, which cannot be touched at all prior to a shot. Apparently the "waste" in waste bunker, according to Sweet, indicates the wasted effort of the golf course architect to actually impose a challenge there. Upon the ruling, in the following year's GBI, which had subsequently experienced a real influx of top-shelf tour personalities, players all aimed for the waste bunker of course, each improving their lie and looking like bakers to each personal cake in the process, the par-4 playing to a stroke average of 3.14 that year with three players making eagle from "Camp Shopiere." Sweet wonders: "Christ with a visor on! What the hell is happening to us?"

Sweet set his bag down at arrival to his ball, which was buoyed so nicely by a particularly lush piece of fairway that it seemed to almost levitate. They waited for Blurry to hit.

Sweet knew about Conny's caddying history and honored it sincerely. He continued to speak hushed and quickly, with the pines still picking it up and reverberating.

"There is nothing else like the caddy tradition, anywhere, and God keep them at the clubs and on the Seniors (Champions) Tour, but all I'm saying is if professional golf continues to build advantage after advantage for already supremely talented people, where does it decide to give the golf course a chance to come into play again? When does 'par' get to mean something again? How great is it, really, that these guys are able to shoot 63 nowadays? Of course the first thought is to lengthen the courses. Just add *more*. But what if they just carried their own bag?"

Given the population explosion, Sweet doesn't see 8,000- and 9,000-yd. courses continuing to be a viable option. And don't these guys know that it isn't the scoring, but the competition between golfers that intrigues audiences? Golf could be one very simple step away from beating greed and ugliness to the punch and conversely pumping a magnum of stamen zing back into the game.

"Maybe the newest challenge could come from the walking part."

"Clark Bar, those guys walk 4-5 rounds a week, in a row, sometimes more than 30 weeks a year."

"I'm saying it would be incredibly difficult."

"An article series?"

"Yeah."

"Can you write, Clark Bar?"

"How the hell should I know."

"I'll make it a pact for the back side."

"Fair enough."

Blurry's second shot on 2: Blurry, ever the tactician, had pulled a 5-iron for his second shot at Triple-the-Pines's shortest par-5 because it is his favorite iron to hit and it would put him at a comfortable approach-shot distance of 100 yds. away from the green. As comfortable as he was with the whole concept, Blurry hit the smoothest 5-iron he had hit all summer, about 180 yds., dead-center fairway, sitting exactly 100 yds. out from the pin. His strategy—Blurry's course management—was weaving itself into the psychic fabric of the foursome.

"What under the sun is that guy up to?" Sweet was still hushed but slower now. Buck could be seen over in the right rough following Blurry's shot all the way from start to finish, then looking back at Blurry, who was still holding his follow-through. "It's like he's thinking." Conny began to block out the concept of Blurry with no cell phone being able to think and possibly winning because if it.

"Alright Clark Bar, let's see it."

Sweet wanted to make up for his double-bogey at The Noose, and while he thought birdie would obviously do that, deep down he knew that par would set him straight too. But here was the 7-handicapper of the group on the easiest hole of the golf course with about 240 yds. to the front of the green. What does it look like for a 7-handicapper to pull out a 6-iron in this situation and lay up comfortably in the fairway, vis-à-vis *Blurry*?

Sweet's second shot on 2: Sweet pulled 5-wood and hoped for the best, knowing that club still gave him no chance to reach the green. Sweet addressed the ball and looked down on the 5-wood, the head looking almost too small to cover the area of a golf ball, and he focused on concentrating on remembering the range. Thinking only of keeping his head still and his eye on the ball, Sweet absolutely laced it, 220 yds. right up the gut, just 20 yds. short of the green in the fairway, with no idea how he pulled it off considering he was almost sullen standing over the shot. Conny thought the surprise on Blurry's face was a bit unbecoming—especially of a 7-handicapper, right?

Turns out that all four men managed to hit the 2nd green in regulation, each man lying 3 on the par-5 and putting for birdie. However, Clark Bar's third shot from only 20 yds. off the green was a good example of one of the many crevices in the Grand Canyon that exists between pros and weekenders—aside from driving distance, driving accuracy, general iron play, putting, devotion to practice, and the will to win—and that's chipping. Clark Bar had a wide open, slightly uphill chip shot, plenty of green to work with between him and the pin, not much break. But he chunked it, the misguided ball finding a nondescript point 18 ft. short of the cup. It stung Clark Bar, and stung deeply, to see Buck get proxie in this instance.

Even though the friendship-jeopardizing Nassau was being played straight up, the handicap-considered Scotch game at a dollar a point was not without intrigue. The guys were still set-tling into their wagers, their faces were not yet weathered by the prospect of losing, nor elastic from points garnered. On the 2nd green, they were still three real estate appraisers and a regional sales manager that had very recently stepped onto a golf course. After a valiant attempt at reaching the green in 2 but winding up in the greenside bunker that's at least six feet deep (one of Phil Black's attempts at a "coffin" bunker), Conny 2-putted for his par in very good fashion, coming from 50 ft. away. On his second putt, Conny did an interesting thing, choosing not to mark and wait after his first putt, but went directly ahead with his second putt, a 6-ft. come-backer, in order to let his partner know where Force 2 From Namino, WI That Is stood before Buck's attempt at birdie. Buck would then know what, exactly, was on the line when it came time to stand over his birdie putt. Conny rolled in the 6-footer, announcing to the rest of the guys that he is not to be taken lightly this day, and giving him the best feeling he had had generally speaking in about three weeks. Blurry also did well to get down in two putts from 30 ft. for his par, having left himself only a 2-ft. tap-in for par. The two oppo-nents were in with pars. So much was riding on their respective partners. Sweet was then faced with 18 footer for birdie and subsequnt delusions of grandeur.

Sweet's putt on 2: Sweet making birdie here stood for four main things, in Sweet's opinion, and he thought about them while over his putt. He thought: 1) it would guarantee that Force 2 From Namino, WI That Is could not break out an umbrella on his and Blurry's collective ass, though if one had to be broken out, this early in the round with so few points available (no presses, yet) isn't the worst place it could happen; not by far, 2) it could in fact put enough pressure on Buck to not only cause him to miss his birdie putt, but to instill the kind of shakes a gambling and alcohol addict could suffer, simultaneously, maybe even inducing versions of visual and auditory hallucinations, things similar to schizophrenia, and delirium tremors, which could definitely cause Buck to 3-putt from 12 ft., 3) it would be a *birdie*, jimmy-rigging a cantilever under Sweet's fainting 7-handicap for the time being, and 4) chances of Sweet having to research the parenting techniques of post-Victorian era parents would ease up a bit. Sweet cleared his mind. Then, the only thought in his head was *get it to the hole*. With a firm stroke the ball rolled cleanly along its chosen line, Sweet bending at the knees in hope, but the break did not come until the ball rolled past the cup, which it did to about 1.5 ft. Sweet tapped in.

"Can't believe it broke after the hole."

"That was a good roll, Clarkie."

Buck almost blacked out from over-stimulus.

Buck's putt on 2: In this kind of situation, Buck often did the math before he putted and math doesn't necessarily promote the clearheadedness that would be best for Buck's putting, even though Buck's actually pretty good at math. Buck calculated: 1) making this birdie putt means Force 2 From Namino, WI That Is get all four points—

1. prox (Buck was closest to the pin in regulation)
2. birdie (if Buck makes the putt)
3. ball (Buck making birdie would also give Force 2 From Namino, WI That Is low ball), and
4. total (Buck making birdie would give Force 2 From Namino, WI That Is low total, 9, to Sweet and Blurry's 10)—

making it 4 = 8 points, the amazing multi-orgasmic umbrella, and a grail. But there was still more math to think about, including 2) that would put Sweet and Blurry down 9 points after only two holes, not a small hole to dig out from and could very easily incite an early press, possibly Buck's *raison d'être*—whether requesting one or accepting one—either way, it meant *more*, and 3) if his birdie putt here does cause Sweet and Blurry to press by, say, the 4th or 5th hole, that means points will at least double for the rest of the front-9, meaning … and 4) *fuck it, just make the fucking putt first*, and 5) it would put him a stroke ahead of Conny and Blurry and two strokes ahead of Sweet on what Buck knew could potentially prove to be a friendship-ending Nassau.

Of course this was too much going on in the old noggin, so Buck mustered his powers of concentration, recent gargantuan Old Style wearing off as it was. From 12 ft. away, his putt would break right to left somewhere between 6-8 in. depending on the speed he gave the ball. It's a definite gonads-check, this kind of putt, especially when it's for an umbrella-inducing birdie. With Buck, guys could never tell if he was actually ballsy, stupid, shaking, or drunk, but he usually went at these kinds of putts very firmly. Buck's stroke was as good as any professional's on this putt, his head stayed dead still, only his shoulders moving as required by the length of the putt, and he gave it plenty of speed. No way it was going to be left short of the cup. The ball moved so quickly over the 12 ft. and so smoothly into the hole that it looked as though it had scurried to do so, like a white rodent suddenly caught between three real estate appraisers and a regional sales manager, scared shitless and in search of its hole. It happened so quickly that it did not afford Buck the time to dramatically react to the umbrella-garnering putt. He just looked up at Conny who was like *what the hell just happened* then over to Sweet and Blurry who were like *no way that just happened.* The surprise did not allow Buck to let out a whoomp or a fist-pump, and he knew that to try to do so now would be awkward, half-hearted, so he just gracefully walked to the hole and retrieved his ball with a smile, and the foursome exited the 2nd green as though it was a place they had come to for the first time, looked around, and moved on.

Those who mockingly refer to the smaller marsh that comes into play on this hole as "Black's Bog" due to greenskeeper Phil Black's unfortunate late-night mishap with a front-end loader here will obtain a keener understanding of karma as they walk off the 12th green only to find that the 13th hole is engulfed by even more of it.
—*Chicago Golf*

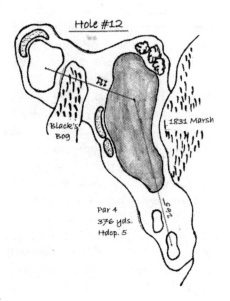

Blurry sidled up to Conny.

"What's up, Bro-heimer."

"You're looking good this morning, Blurry."

"Lot of golf left to be played."

"Always."

"What about developing a web site that reports only good news?"

"Say again."

"What about developing a web site that reports only good news, and if it became popular enough, look into developing print, radio, and TV versions?"

"A web site?"

"To start. It would only report good news, and it would never be allowed to report studies, surveys, reports, or polls that are not 100% conclusive. Like tangibly."

"You want this as a pact?"

"I've been taking those FastPage web site development classes up at Halcyon Community. Let's just say I would do it if I lost a bet."

"A web site."

"I might just call it The Good News. And when people asked about it, they would say 'So, what's The Good News?'"

"The news isn't always good, Tom."

"No. In fact, that's my point. Good news could be such a rare commodity that I could create an incredible niche in the industry."

"What industry?"

"The news industry. The entertainment industry. You know, the media industry. Let's face it, we've got the bad news pretty much covered. People always complain about all the bad news and what about the good news but nobody does a damn thing about it. I always thought that was weird. I mean, even your media mogul who could give two shits about whether the news is good or bad or not must realize the revenue generating potential of offering something that nobody else does. Something people seem to crave."

"What, like goodnews.com? utopiandelusion.com?"

Blurry and Conny were making their way towards their golf balls, each having gone up the left side of the 3rd hole, each avoiding the "ravine" that comes into the heart of the fairway. Blurry, again taking 3-wood off the tee and again reaping the reward of adhering to his commitment to course management, his ball landing in the left rough just off the fairway. Conny's ball was about 30 yds. past Blurry, also left rough. Buck, fueled by his conservative approach to birdie on the previous hole, took 3-iron off the tee to completely take the ravine out of play, which looks good on paper, except that an apparent lack of focus resulted from Buck's thinking he was taking an easier route via the 3-iron and a lackluster swing produced a thinly hit ball, putting it up the right side of the fairway only about 150 yds., leaving him an approach shot of at least 225 yds. Sweet had probably the best drive of the group, having put it into the middle of the small strip of fairway to the left of the ravine.

As Buck, Blurry, and Sweet began to prepare for their approach shots, respectively, Conny made his way past them all and towards his ball, which took him past the ravine by about 15 yds. and into the corner of the dog-leg on the left side, giving Conny an unobstructed view of the entire hole from tee to green. While he waited for the guys to hit up, Conny looked back at the tee box that was nestled among the pines and how they shaped the hole down both sides to the bend and how they curved around him on the left side so that, given the precise spot he was standing in and the way he was facing, it felt like they the pines were curving his shoulders inwardly for Conny, very much like a hug from behind, and Conny thought about the irony of a tree hugging a human in this day and age. He followed the remainder of the 3rd hole until the oaks took over down the rest of it, along both sides of the green and where they ran into Blind Creek behind the green. He grew anxious to hit his approach.

Conny's approach shot on 3: With about 120 yds. to the pin that was tucked somewhat dastardly in the back-left upper-tier portion of the green, and with a picture in his mind of Phil Black sipping good hot coffee in the clubhouse and explaining red position flags, Conny realized he was between clubs here. (That is, the 120-yd. length was too short for wedge and too long for sandwedge; this would require either playing it safe with sandwedge to the front of the green or attempting a ¾-swing with wedge out of the rough, which, for Conny, when trying ¾-swings from anywhere, the word *unpredictable* will flash before his eyes afterwhich the word *understatement* will follow and somehow laughingly as only visions of words can sometimes do.) It was too early in the round to take risks. Conny pulled sandwedge, played for the front half of the green, and with what is a relatively patented smooth stroke with sandwedge, Conny put just a great move on the ball, caught it flush, and the ball flew torque-minded from the juicy rough and continued to fly with a slight draw until it landed on the back tier of the green about 2 yds. short of the back edge and stuck there, app. 10 ft. from the hole.

"Man that thing flew" Conny said outloud even though Buck, Blurry, and Sweet splayed out 80 yds. in front of him, all over the place.

"Golf shot, Con-stance!"

"Consistently Golfing Bro-mide!"

Up at the green, Conny sat 10 ft. away for birdie, while the rest of the group sat further away for par after mediocre chip shots. Sweet was down near the front of the green after having chipped out from the oaks. Sweet hit his first putt with way too much speed to compensate for getting over the tier, and the ball raced past the difficult cup placement until it came to rest against the fringe of the rough, 15 ft. past the cup.

Sweet ambling up to the back tier of the green gave the group time to think, which isn't helpful at all, usually. Spreadsheets did flash before each man's particular mind depicting the ramifications of that day's Nassau for them and also depicting a little bit of their mind. Buck O'Royerson's mental spreadsheet, for example, was color-coded. It also came with a little animated helper, only instead of the little assistant being, say, a paper clip riding a magic carpet of a piece of paper or something to that effect, Buck's animated guide was an old drunken land-locked long shoreman, a sort of grizzled sea-farer with baggy pants who smelled foul and wore specks and buckled shoes, and the frills of his scarf were in tatters. Buck's guide did nothing to aid in guiding him through his mental spreadsheet though. In fact, as opposed to standard animated assistants that will pop up and ask *What would you like to do?*, Buck's elfin auditor would pop up, somehow crackling, shove his hands in his baggy pockets, shrug his shoulders and say *Christ with a 7-wood! What in the hell do YOU want?*:

| "If I Lose" by William O'Royerson ||
Opponent	Pact
Conny:	I would have to run for city council, and I think I could win it. This town has gotten so damn out of hand with development and bullshit I don't even recognize it anymore and I really hate it. So does everybody else I know. It's getting dirty and ugly and crowded. People are bummed and even kind of scared, and it doesn't even have anything to do with race. I have to **think** about driving across town now it's so damn crowded. I know I administered an ungodly portion of the loans necessary to build residential and commercial infrastructure, but I want it to stop now. On the other hand, I don't want to lose to Bro-mide. I wonder if anybody on city council likes to get high …
Blurry:	**D-CODE?** OK, Bromenn, like you never took a drink in your life. Give me a break with this pact. You smoked more hookah in college than Peter Tosh. (I wonder if Peter Tosh went to college …) You always had the best hookah, and to this day you were the funnest person I ever did shrooms with. You still drink like a fish. So get off your high horse.
Sweet:	Junior college scholarship. That's really not so ridiculous. It's an excellent idea, in fact. I would love to be the judge of an essay contest.

Sweet's mental spreadsheet was also animated, but in a way that was completely unrelated to the content of the spreadsheet. That is, it had stars that shot across it because Sweet had just watched an episode the night before about comets on TLC and the History Channel had an episode about how the Great Chicago Fire may have been started via a meteor shower. So Sweet's spreadsheet had shooting stars. Other than that, it looked like your average DuKeefe Mortgage Corp. spreadsheet:

What Losing Could Mean To A Clark Sweet	
Opponent	**Pact**
Conny:	Save Girl Scout Island? No way, Bro. No way. Come on.
Blurry:	OK, I have to admit, I think discipline should probably be reintroduced to your average child, and even to adolescents. But how the hell should I know how parents raised the WWII generation? I know they didn't have to deal with TV. Common sense parenting. I wonder if Conny saw my son Tim's name in the police report in the *Chronicle* two months ago … By way, why would a kid break into somebody's garage to steal two bikes when he has two of his own, anyway? Huh... Well, no way I want to have to take that on though.
Oh, Drunkagain?:	I bet Buck doesn't even know what *biodegradable* means. Biodegradable means that it can decompose without having to use fire…

Blurry's mental spreadsheet was clear as a bell. It was organized. It was color-coded, but only in various shades of blue. It was all related only to the pacts themselves. It read like collateral sales material that was trying to sell Blurry's pacts—to Blurry. It appeared to Blurry in complete form and did not waver until he chose to think about something else. The entire time it appeared to Tom, he could hear his cell phone not ringing:

***LOSING*—And How It Can Work for Tom Blair**	
Opponent	**Pact**
Conny:	**Habitat for Humanity** Since 1976, Habitat has built more than 50,000 houses with families throughout the United States and another 100,000-plus houses in communities around the world. Now at work in 92 countries, they are building a house every 26 minutes. By 2005, Habitat houses will be sheltering 1 million people. ~~(I have no business working with this organization. I don't want to.)~~
Blurry:	**Recycling** In an integrated waste management system, any recycling program should work with other recycling efforts to remove valuable commodities from the "waste stream." How a community chooses to do this will vary. Individual communities have personalities and what works for one community will not necessarily work for another. Consider:

	• Drop-off/Donation centers • Buyback centers Markets for the recycled materials are of main concern. Not all recyclables have market values that make recycling worth the cost for a community. Market development must be explored on the consumer, manufacturing, and governmental levels.
	Recycling is a choice for everyone. Increasingly, communities are beginning to make the choice to participate. Individuals will always have the choice to treat their used items as trash or as resources. ~~(Somebody would help me with this, right?)~~
Oh,Drunkagain?:	**Physio-'Neers** Ever see that refrigerator magnet that reads "The hurrier I go, the behinder I get"? I guess that's what Physio-'Neers means to me… ~~(Um, this ain't gonna work.)~~

Conny's spreadsheet probably should have covered all 36 pacts and the ramifications for all of the guys involved, but it didn't. It only covered what would happen to Conny should he lose on the front-9. This was because guys were approaching Conny with secret new ideas for pacts and also because Conny really didn't have 36 pacts at the ready, he had lied, he didn't know what he was going to do about pacts for the back-9 and total-18, and so guys coming up with their own ideas for pacts really worked for Conny for two reasons: 1) guys were volunteering, and 2) they were filling in the blanks. Despite what was missing from it, Conny's spreadsheet was the color of early morning sunshine and its grid was outlined in electric blue:

| Conny Bromenn's Intense Desire To Not Lose ||
Opponent	Pact
Sweet:	Will my ego allow me to lose to Sweet? I am going to begin an awareness campaign for the commercial-free Masters, and it's main objective is going to be to unmask the PGA's seemingly indifferent attitude towards a commercial-free tournament, and a major at that. How can they not possibly tout the benefits of this, daily? Why do we not hear more about this, and why doesn't TV anticipate it more robustly? We're talking about hours and hours in a row of free television without commercial interruption. How can the PGA not outwardly embrace an idea so good for its own game? How can it not promote the same idea for further tournaments? How can the major influx of golf news right now be either infomercials for the Perfect Club®, the Inside Swing®, or web sites for Elin Nordegren, when there should be a weekly remembrance of how The Masters is commercial-free? Seriously, isn't it strange that this doesn't receive more attention, all things considered? I will be happy to answer these questions, but **do I really have to lose to Sweet in order to do it?**
Blurry:	OK, here's the deal on comparing the thrill/learning experience of turning Amish vs. space travel, in a nutshell: • Turning Amish would introduce app. 80% of us to the Earth, which has app. infinite number of life forms, whereas space is a dead vacuum. You know it is. • Space travel spends hundreds of billions of dollars on exploring places where we can't live, nor would we want to. We are earthlings, and that's just how it is. Also, the cop-out that space exploration is trying to afford us so that we can indeed eventually kill Earth, you know, just shit on it and move on, is too large of a cop-out as to be truly comprehended. Plus it's really just about garnering more real estate for more money for the powers that be. You know it. • Not only would we experience the fascination of how our planet works and work primarily outdoors, the money saved could be used to retool our industries for hydrogen fuel cell technology, immediately, like by the end of the year. That's how much money we're talking about here. Many people think the most wasteful characteristic of Americans today is the 3,500 sq. ft. house. It's not. It's space travel. But **do I really have to lose to Blurry to make this point?**
Buck:	Car-pooling. How hard can that be, really? **Losing to Buck is not an option though.**

Blurry and Buck did manage to hit putts that got to the hole, and both displayed quite a deft touch, each winding up with tap-ins for their bogeys and each showing Conny the exact line to take for his putt. Sweet, his ball on the fringe of the green but leaning against the cut of rough that borders it, decided that as a 7-handicapper he was called upon to do something creative here, something of skill, since the rough would definitely get in the way of a putter.

Sweet's second "putt" on 3: "Blading" a sandwedge (using your sandwedge as a putter essentially by stroking the ball at its equator with the very bottom edge of a sandwedge, which, when done correctly can get a ball rolling as smoothly as with a putter, sometimes even more so in a weird kind of way) is an option in a scenario like this, but blading a sandwedge is not something that has any margin for error, margins for error being major components of Clark Bar's game. Clarkie's actually practiced this shot a few times before while goofing around on the practice green though, so it's not like he's completely unaware of the concepts and procedures involved here. He's actually done it before, and he decided to *trust* that. *Trust what you did right that one time that you did do it right. Aim for the hole and believe in yourself.* Clark took some very studied practice strokes, brushing the tips of rough with the very bottom of his sandwedge, then adjusting himself to address his ball, all of which he did just like they do on TV. He choked up on the club and his practice strokes had been almost identical to his normal putting stroke (instead of a chipping stroke). Most importantly, he fought the notion that he would, for some reason, have to stroke the ball harder since it was up against rough and on the fringe and he was using a wedge and hitting the ball at its equator—he ignored all that. He was simply putting from about 15 ft. away to save par. Sweet thought about the feel of a 15-ft. putt, kept his eye on the ball, trusted his stroke, decided he actually wanted to make this shot, his last thought being *trust*. After realizing that he had not heard a cell phone in almost 30 min., Sweet bladed his sandwedge so purely that the ball rolled possibly more distinctly than it does when Sweet uses a putter a lot of the time, traversing the 2 ft. of fringe without wavering then finding actual solace in the green, tracking, oh God was it tracking, right up until the ball caught the left half of the cup in a way that made the cup look like it had stretched to receive Sweet's ball, the ball rolling and traversing like a leaf on a creek that suddenly gets pulled asunder, the cup indeed swallowing it.

"I can't believe my own eyes."

"Well done, Clark Bar!"

Sweet was redeemed then. Almost forever.

Conny's putt on 3: Conny can't feel more solid over a putt than he did here, and even though he had been feeling solid over almost all of his shots so far, he knew that was not an automatic bid for actual success. Having gotten an education from Buck and Blurry, Conny had the line on this 10-footer, he definitely knew the line, so it was going to be a matter of starting the ball out on that line and giving it the proper speed. Just get it started and get it to the hole. Conny wanted to do good things in life and improve himself, but he would be damned if he was going to lose to these chumps in order to do those things. On the other hand, he could not help but to be enthusiastic about his pacts, sometimes even outwardly. Conny making birdie here would put Buck and Blurry 2 strokes back, Sweet 3 strokes off, and would put Conny in the driver's seat as far as winning the Nassau on the front side. But Conny had heard rumors that Hootie Johnson was entertaining offers from potential commercial sponsors again for The Masters, and Conny wanted so desperately to try to persuade Hootie not to revert to a sponsored Masters—don't give in, Hootie—to see the utter majesty of that tournament with no commercial interruption, the revolution that that is. Conny's desire to make a difference with Hootie Johnson had a neutralizing effect; i.e., losing the Nassau meant Conny would get to do something he was passionate about, and this took every possible twinge out of his putting stroke, knowing that missing and losing meant he would get to experience passion so he was ridiculously relaxed and stroked the 10-footer like a star on tour. The ball had absolutely no chance of escaping the cup. The guys watched the ball heading straight for the hole, hugging the green, tracking, not a spike mark or imperfection to cause malfunction, the ball rolling perfectly into the hole as though it was home and happy to be there.

Buck, for one, went through so many emotions, beginning with 1) Conny's birdie being the last remaining component of another umbrella-opener for Force 2 (*NOTE: To garner a point for birdie in these guys' version of the Scotch game, it had to be a "natural" birdie; that is, a par could not become birdie were a player to get a stroke on that hole*) but 2) it also put Conny ahead in the friendship-endangering Nassau, but 3) the umbrella would surely have to induce a press from Blurry and Sweet, and early, and 4) this was Buck's grail over all. Force 2 had opened a second umbrella in a row, which had never been done before by this foursome. Conny was conflicted too, at even par and on his way to shooting if not breaking 75 for sure, while his opportunity to save The Masters and the Earth began to whither a bit.

Commonly referred to by locals as "Jason"—to the tune of *Friday the 13th*—one is almost obligated to note while standing on the tee box that the hole often plays "dead" into the wind. And so it does. The saving grace of the hole, ironically, is that the wind will help hold the long-iron or fairway wood often necessary to reach the green. Apparently, if the northern Illinois winds are blowing hard enough, they can even help hold a knock-down driver.

—*Chicago Golf*

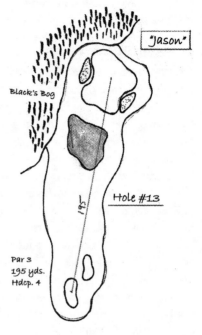

"Jason"

Black's Bog

Hole #13

195

Par 3
195 yds.
Hdcp. 4

Over 4.5 hours, walking a golf course develops a certain rhythm. Walking is what makes it impossible for Conny to keep songs out of his head over 18 holes. "Rio" does pop in every now and then and usually signifies a high energy level, though not always conducive to the best frame of golf-mind. "Rio" needs to be monitored, or it can overtake the game at hand. "Rio" can be harnessed, though. "Billie Jean" is usually a given, and Conny figures his healthy stride somehow suits that beat, because it can come out of nowhere. Others that get a lot of play include "Get Back" "Holiday" and "Locomotive Breath." "Goin' Back to Cali" has been a favorite. "De Do Do Do, De Da Da Da" was in such heavy rotation at one time that the song simply would not dissipate or even frag*ment* during any waking hours, which began to concern Conny. The ability of "De Do Do Do, De Da Da Da" to help him break 80 aside, its omnipresence seemed too implausible to live with over time, and the failure of certain measures taken by Conny to subdue it was unnerving. When the playing of "De Do Do Do, De Da Da Da" itself cranked on the stereo several times in a row one night at home did not work, Conny decided to go get drunk down the street at Cathy's Tavern, not so much as a measure to ward off "De Do Do Do, De Da Da Da" as it was to just release the stress associated with carrying it around everywhere. In other words, he just figured he'd go get drunk *with* "De Do Do Do, De Da Da Da." He happened to walk into Cathy's Tavern just as someone lit up "Give It To Me, Baby" on the jukebox, which, even without any beer yet, interceded between Conny and "De Do Do Do, De Da Da Da" quite successfully.

Be that as it may, the power of song to propel a golfer should not be underestimated, and the power of walking to ignite song is incendiary. Overall in music as it relates to golf, some songs are "beat" songs that come via walking and they help maintain an excellent rhythm, and some songs are "motivational" and help to keep a positive message going in a player's head. "Amber" is an example of a song that did both for Conny. Unfortunately, not all songs if stuck in one's head will provide the right rhythm or the right message (much less both) necessary to maintain the cadence of a well-played round of golf. They can be disproportionately energizing. Conny has mentioned "Barracuda," "Dirty Deeds," and "Immigrant Song" in this category.

Even if you took away walking's ability to ignite song, walking would still be the most important factor in golf. It must be so overtly characteristic to the game walking must be because it is so completely overlooked as golf's heart. Walking is certainly golf's major challenge and its ultimate pleasure. Everything that happens during 18 holes is born from walking.

For the weekender, though, it is getting more and more difficult now to walk. In possibly one of the grossest forms of unchecked greed, golf courses and golf course architecture are restricting walking completely and offering only cart-taking as an option. They are being built golf courses are around cart paths, pavement mind you, in order for rounds to be played quicker allowing more people to "get through" the course in a day. "Higher turnover." This isn't particularly a new phenomenon, but it is rampant now. And alarming. Many courses today, and this is flat out disgusting, charge the same amount for walking a round as they do for riding a cart. To discourage walking, that's why. But carts will never look truly at home on a golf course. For the sake of those that are unable to make the walk but still enjoy the fresh air and can put a decent move on the ball, carts aren't really hurting anybody. But for those that are fully able to make the walk and choose a cart anyway, especially those that just assume that is the procedure, there is nary a more heartbreaking example of carpe diem gone utterly to waste.

This hole kicks off Dog-Leg Run, where four out of the five remaining holes are dog-legs, some of which are quite severe and two will bring North Pond into play not untreacherously. It is important to do what you can to take advantage of the 14th hole's downhill, down-wind allowances, if only to be able to face the remainder of Dog-Leg Run with some form of optimism, which is crucial.
—*Chicago Golf*

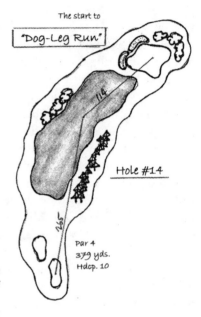

The start to

"Dog-Leg Run"

Hole #14

Par 4
379 yds.
Hdcp. 10

Marti Lynn Morely loves men, which is a highly sought after quality in a beverage cart woman. A beverage cart woman who has been let's say scorned and is bitter and does *not* like the fact that she is scorned and bitter (as opposed to the beverage cart woman who, twisted, may actually like that) will not enjoy a day on the golf course serving beverages to men, there's just no way. It being on the early side of 10:30 AM, Marti Lynn was just testing out her beverage cart, but she knew full well that there was more than one group on the course that would have a beer right now. That there was more than one foursome that was probably looking for her. One or two golfers might be desperate, actually. Witness Buck O'Royerson making large Xs with his arms above his head with a large white towel in one hand after spotting Marti Lynn's amber-hair siren, waving down Marti Lynn like a castaway to a search plane.

"My favorite foursome at the head of the pack!"

"Ms. Morely."

"Four draughts of your finest lager, if you would, lady."

"How 'bout four Old Styles?"

"Perfect."

Marti Lynn truly did not smile if she didn't mean it. The site of the guys in early-round froth and obviously with a few things on their minds incited her to smile.

"How's business?" Buck paid for an Old Style. "Don't be a stranger."

"The place is starting to fill up fast. They got Pogo on the run."

Beers and money and pleasantries were exchanged promptly so as not to lose pace. It was a small break, but everybody who was a part of it was able to carefully surmise each other during it, Marti Lynn possibly more acutely than anybody else since she had not been hiking over the last few holes and had absolutely no fatigue factor. Quite the opposite. She was just beginning to burgeon in the morning. She had definitely sensed something different in these four and her hand downright slid from creamy aurae when exchanging beers for money with them. Marti Lynn thanked the gentlemen for their business and gratuity and assured them (while looking at Buck) that she would not leave them to parch in the middle of Triple-the-Pines. And she was gone in an instant, diving into the viridescence.

Guys began calculating yardage for the par-3 4th hole in different ways. Blurry found the sprinklerhead that had yardage on it (163) near the front of the tee box and walked off 8 yds. from there back to where Phil Black's crew had placed the blue tees; Sweet walked to the very front of the tee box and threw up some grass to check for wind, which is something Sweet has been doing since he saw Tiger Woods do it that way at Medinah in 1999; Conny gauged the wind too, though with far less mimicry than

Sweet, and walked off the yardage to the sprinklerhead for himself; Buck inhaled half his Old Style then asked Conny what the yardage was.

"171 to the middle, pin looks a little back left, really no wind. I'm gonna say 175." Conny's tone signaled the new depths the competition was beginning to explore. The weight of pacts began to settle in. For Sweet and Blurry, the weight of a dollar a point in the Scotch game wasn't particularly light, either. What had been a relatively congenial walk-along had very suddenly become *what have we gotten ourselves into*. Some teeth actually gnashed.

Par-3s are not considered to be the best places to press. There's too much that could go right/wrong too quickly, and if your team's looking to press, that often means the other team probably has momentum on their side, something you may not want to mess with on a par-3. Even though Sweet and Blurry were down 17 points this early in the match, it *was* still early in the match and there was no need for them to get anxious; it wouldn't particularly behoove them to press here on the first par-3 at Triple-the-Pines, then have to live with the press for the rest of the front-9.

Blurry and Sweet agreed to press, of course. Patience not a real big virtue with a lot of the guys. Buck did a jig but kept his Old Style steady. Conny was teeing his ball up, 7-iron in hand, and he stood back to view the 4th hole as it hugged the northern woods, Blind Creek crossing it at the middle and disappearing one way into Triple-the-Pines and one way into the woods. He was even-par after 3 holes, one of those holes being the toughest on the course, and he and Buck were already amassing a considerable bounty.

Birdying the 3rd hole came with the responsibility of "honors" for Conny on the 4th tee. ("Honors" is a system by which the golfer with the best score on the previous hole gets to hit first off the next tee, golfers then hitting in succession of how they scored on that previous hole, best to worst. Having honors is kind of a stamen-enlivener because it shows that you scored better than anybody else on the previous hole, which, your ego's got to love that. If there is a tie for best score on a hole, the golfer who had honors before that hole retains honors, and if you asked most golfers to be honest they would have to admit that tying for best score on a hole but still retaining honors somehow oddly makes them feel like they still achieved the best score on the tied hole. Honors comes with a miniature glory like that.) In the case of the 4th hole (and most par-3s), having honors also comes with a guinea pig effect in that you will be the first to test whether your yardage/wind/club selection/gonads-check calculations are in sync. Conny would be that guinea pig here on the 4th. The other three golfers get to observe what is basically an experiment and their observations help them to hone a research-based shot of their own, with the fourth player to hit having had the most research to work from, at which point only his swing can get in the way.

The struggle between wanting to uphold pacts like saving The Masters and the Earth and wanting to shoot 75 and beat guys bloody for money continued to effect a neutrality in Conny so relaxing that he could actively consider the relaxation and that still wouldn't upset his being relaxed. The kind of balance that Conny was experiencing then usually comes with description reserved for Zen garden meditation. Conny could feel the struggle within him but that it was a struggle that had no losing end, to the point that, really, deep down, losing would be winning for Conny that day—the ultimate win/win situation, his desire to save The Masters and the Earth being so strong. This was going on inside Conny as he stood over his ball on the 4th tee. He could feel his worn cleats grip the tee box under him, he was so damn in tune.

Conny's tee shot on 4: Almost implausibly neutral, Conny took the club back, thought only about keeping his eye on the ball—that was his single thought—brought the club through steely-eyed and the clubface of the 7-iron harmonized with the turf and the ball, and the harmony came up through the shaft and into Conny's hands and rolled up his arms and into his cranium until it overwhelmed his heart and stamen. The ball fired out of the chute formed by trees on both sides of the 4th tee, it dissected the chute, then catapulted from a second booster propulsion that took it up and drew it (eased it left) over the large bunker that guarded the front left side of the green, where it then stuck to the green and danced a bit, settling about 15 ft. left of the pin.

Conny's shot was so well executed that anyone watching it would never have noticed how much trouble a golf ball can get into on this par-3; Conny's ball transcended all that. The other guys had hoped to learn something from Conny's tee shot, but they had no chance whatsoever of being able to identify with a 7-iron from that yardage struck that well. Since Conny's shot could not really be considered by the rest of the group and because Buck was next to hit, Buck, for all intents and purposes, would become the new pissed off guinea pig by which Blurry and Sweet would conduct their research.

"That was pretty, Con-found-it."

"I give it 9.5 on the Bro-mometer."

"You can't designate something on a meter, dumb ass, it designates it for you."

"You're so damn smart, show us how to hit this shot then O'Royerson."

Squatting several ft. behind where he had marked his ball, Conny studied the line of his upcoming birdie attempt. (When your ball is on the green, you are allowed to "mark" it, primarily to get it out of the way of other players' lines, but also so that you can clean the ball—you are not allowed to change golf balls at that time, however—and any flat round object is acceptable to use as a marker, such as a coin or a 30-day Serenity Found chip, as examples.) From there, Conny would get a comprehensive review of the short game of the standard 11-handicapper: Blurry's tee shot had landed short of the bunker, so he would be attempting a "flop" shot of sorts (a flop shot being an attempt to get a ball to pop up in the air quickly over a short distance then land softly, usually employed in situations where there is some form of trouble between you and the hole, e.g., bunker, water, more shitty rough, etc.); Buck was in the trap in front of the green; and Sweet was about 5 yds. right of the green in the rough, a good 40 ft. from the pin, where he would have to make a choice between a standard chip shot with sandwedge or a "bump-and-run" shot that might call for a 7- or 8-iron to help run the 40-ft. distance.

Sweet's chip shot on 4: Sweet pulled 8-iron and attempted a bump-and-run and did so as a 7-handicapper who lies about his ability. After thinking *stroke it like you would a putter* and *don't take your eye off the ball*, Sweet's last thought before bringing his 8-iron through the ball was *Blurry doesn't have his cell phone*, which he thought was a weird thought for him to have. But there must have been something to it because upon impact Sweet's ball popped out of the rough, rode the break of the tier nicely right to left as though Sweet had calculated it to do so (which is possible, in all fairness), found its way over the tier and towards the hole, and nestled comfortably about 2.5 ft. from the hole. Though it's possible Sweet has never executed the bump-and-run so successfully, his initial thought as the ball came to rest was still about Blurry's missing cell phone.

"Well done, Clarkie."

"A Sweet shot indeed."

"Are you kidding me with that bump-and-run?"

Sweet tapped in.

Blurry's flop shot on 4: Blurry was next to go and, after surveying the bunker between him and the green, the last thought he had before executing his flop shot was *I don't have my cell phone*, and the exaggeratedly open clubface of his sandwedge came through the ball with assuredness, lofting the ball straight up, floating it over the bunker, it landed like a marshmallow, rolled about 6 ft. and left Blurry with a 5-footer for his par.

"Blurry!"

"Nice shot, Mickelson."

Buck's bunker shot on 4: Buck's turn then, and having seen all the success around him, he was afire. With his ball sitting up well in the trap and on an uphill lie, this was as basic a bunker shot as one could hope for. (Phil Black had constructed a few greenside bunkers just this way, so that, yes, they were hazards to be reckoned with but if you landed in them, they would offer up "easy" bunker shots. Phil did this in order to take pleasure in watching golfers hit bad bunker shots from lies that could not get any easier to hit bunker shots from. Phil is like that, often-times.) Buck dug his feet into the sand, anchored himself, and as he looked at a spot one inch behind the ball, his last thought before impact on that area was *Blurry doesn't have his cell phone* and the ball popped up out of the trap with a mind of it's own and whose mind wanted desperately to find the hole, which it damn near did but stopped about 8 in. in front of the cup, dead on line. Putt conceded.

"What the hell?" Conny spoke out loud.

"Shot, Bucko!"

"Damn thing almost went in."

With Buck and Sweet already in for par and Blurry with probably a little better than a 50-50 chance from 5 ft. away, the indifference in Conny that had made him an electric golfing machine balked briefly due to human wonder. Conny's making par here suddenly carried no weight, even after his expert tee shot into the green. What he thought would be a comprehensive review of the short game of the standard 11-handicapper full of miscues and hearty disgruntlement and bogies had turned into a clinic on how to play three of the most demanding shots around the green, exactly, as they are performed without a cell phone on anyone's person. If Blurry were to make his putt and Conny were to miss his birdie try and make par, nothing would be gained in the Nassau and only one point (1=2 with the press) would be garnered in the Scotch game, that being for prox, and that being all Conny would get for the trouble of striking a 7-iron from 175 yds. like a star on tour. Birdie, however, well that meant "awholefuckingother thing" as Buck was quick to point out, though conflicted, while Conny sized up the putt. Blurry seemed eerily unfazed and drank some beer.

Conny wanted to make this putt, so his previously neutralized body took on actual desire, which was sure to cause a paper jam in his fax machine, so to speak. Making birdie would not put that much of a dent in the Nassau since the guys were looking to make par from all points. But birdie could be a third umbrella in a row, worth 4=8=16 in the currently pressed (once) Scotch game. Birdie here meant Conny could have the best of both worlds, he could make this putt and still not lose too much danger of having to consider pacts while at the same time beating Sweet and Blurry bloody for money. This gave way to unbridled want, jeaopardizing the almost narcotic neutrality.

Conny's putt on 4: As Conny aligned putter to ball, he thought about his initial goal for the day—to break 75. He thought about the taste for the jugular and did he have it, the jugular belonging to the throat of Triple-the-Pines, the course that inevitably seemed to bar him from breaking 80 all summer, the golf course always the true opponent. *Break 75 and then assess the carnage.* Conny took one last look for alignment and, as he kept his head very still, just as he made impact his final thought was *Blurry doesn't have his cell phone* and the ball began tracking for the cup immediately, possibly before it had actually left the face of the putter. The ball levitated along its path and was so unmistakably on line that Conny, not the showboat normally, began to follow his putt as it made its way toward the hole in showboat cockiness and he was preparing a fist pump. The ball got swallowed up and he let out a pump and a whoomp so primal and blind that the rest of the guys couldn't possibly take it personaly, it so obviously came from some other deep-seated source of repression.

"Partner!" Hell with the crazy Nassau, the money was the first thing Buck thought of.

"Great putt, Con-man." Sweet spoke purely out of golf's obligation to etiquette.

Blurry just sort of chortled. He then moved quickly to his own putt, quickly to stem the tsunami that was Conny and Force 2 From Namino, WI That Is.

Blurry's putt on 4: Stunned, yet moving as though he had a secret intent, as though he literally knew something that other guys did not, Blurry's attention to this putt seemed odd. It's important to understand that no matter how often this particular foursome plays together, so many things get forgotten in the heat of battle, even if it is the same battle one hundred times over and no matter how distinctly rules get laid out on the 1st tee. To be fair to this group, however, July 28, 2003 was not the same old battle. It was a battle so varied and rich in its content as to make it new, and throwing something new at these guys—who already forget so many aspects to already timeworn battles—was sure to test their attention to detail. Watching him squat and read his 5-footer from 3 different angles, then get over his putt with downright intensity, it dawns on the guys: *Blurry gets a stroke here.* Blurry making his par putt here would not only save him a stroke in the pacts-injected Nassau, it means a lot to the Scotch game since it would prevent a third umbrella in a row being opened up on his ass by Force 2, saving him and Sweet 15 points. (*NOTE: In these guys' version of the Scotch game, a "net" birdie can tie a natural birdie **if** an umbrella is at stake.*) Blurry stood quite firm over his ball, looked twice between his ball and the hole, felt the weight of his belt as it weighs without a cell phone clipped on to it, and drove the 5-footer home as if he knew exactly what he was doing the whole time.

"That's my damn partner!"

"Solid, Tom."

"Big save there, Blurry. Big save."

Blurry's putt was indeed huge, but Conny's birdie here was still intimidating. Buck couldn't help but share a private moment with his partner as they led the way through the patch of north woods that separates the 4th green and the 5th tee, Force 2 muttering something to each other with not so subtle head-bobs and hand gesticulation that added up to little violent reenactments of Conny's birdie putt, along with definite notation that Force 2 had almost opened up three umbrellas in a row on their asses. As the guys paced through the woods, their tree-acoustic walk exaggerated Force 2's whispers and Sweet and Blurry's silence, simultaneously. Neither Sweet nor Blurry had the wherewithal to note the irony in their approaching The Calm Before the Storm, the collective name for the generous 5th and 6th holes, ironic seeing as how Conny was already a tsunami.

Considered one of the most architecturally sound holes on the course, the 15th is also one of its most scenic as it sits near the center of Triple-the-Pines. It has been said that the idyllic scenery, however, has absolutely no meditative recompense at all for the stress this hole can induce.

—*Chicago Golf*

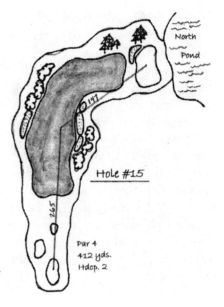

North Pond

Hole #15

197

265

Par 4
412 yds.
Hdcp. 2

The guys could see other guys populating the holes behind them moving at an even pace, growing in numbers, all of them walking. Conny, Buck, Sweet, and Blurry embarked from the tee box out into the 5th hole looking like four lubricated parts under one invisible housing. Tommy Sheehan's foursome was the group nearest behind them as they were just coming off the 3rd tee box, Tommy twirling his club. Though all the guys on the course were living their private, sometimes horribly disjointed golf-lives at that instant, they were moving well as a big operation.

"So, tell us Bro, you must have some pacts in order for the back-9."

"Let's hear some."

"Con-tractually Binding Bro-mide."

"If this is your way of throwing me off while I'm 1-under and fervent, I'm afraid you'll have to do better than that."

"Since you have them all 'at the ready' I believe your term for it was, I see no reason why you can't share a few."

"You're absolutely right. Blurry, if I lose to you on the back-9, I have to campaign for the total, and I mean total, elimination of the Illinois tollway system, and any administration associated or affiliated with it, starting first of course with the Illinois State Toll Highway Authority."

The amount of credibility that Conny had just charged into his off-the-wall Nassau was akin to a bolt of lightning.

"Wow."

"OK."

"OK."

"Conny …"

"Now we're getting somewhere."

"Not if there's a toll booth every 3.5 miles, we're not."

"Right."

"Aren't they already trying to get rid of that?"

"No. In an article in the *Keefe County Chronicle* called "Toll Plan: Brilliant or Crazy? Toll System to Get Bypass Surgery," I read that the Illinois Toll State Highway Authority has a 10-year 'improvement' plan to rebuild 90% of the 274-mile system."

"God, please, not another Illinois Toll Highway State Authority plan. I don't think I can take it. I'm serious."

"Weren't they supposed to get rid of the tolls in 1984?"

"Yes. They promised they would. Not only did they not get rid of them in 1984, but I think they had the unmitigated gall to raise tolls 10 cents that same year. Right up our ass with it. You bet."

"Conny's right. They're going to pay for the rebuilding by increasing tolls big-time for truckers. Plus hikes for people who don't choose to purchase the electronic tollway pass. I read about it in the *Chronicle* in an article called "New Toll House Recipe: Toll Hike Plan Puts Drivers at Fork in Road.""

"Like truckers weren't dangerous enough before. Most of those guys have done actual time. Did you know that?"

"I was once in a very remote part of Washington state and while asking this woman for directions to a less remote part, I asked her if I would need change for tolls on that particular route and she said *what are tolls*. When I told her it was like a booth where you had to pay money to gain access to the road, she said that's like having to pay for access to air to breathe. I had been so programmed all my life by the Illinois Toll Highway Authority State that it wasn't until two days later that I actually agreed with her."

"I'm talking total elimination here. Get the fucking booths out of the middle of the fucking road already. I don't even want the notion to linger."

"It is pretty crazy, if you think about it. Putting something right in the middle of high-speed roads like that. I always thought that that was kind of crazy. Like worse than just 'backwards.' People have been run into and killed at those things, and while throwing $.15 into a basket."

"Blurry's right. Seriously, just tax the residents of the counties that house the tollway and have done with it."

"Bridges. Like major bridges over sounds and canyons I could see paying a toll for."

"Not too many of those in northern Illinois."

"In Washington state, construction of the State Route (SR) 104 Hood Canal Bridge began January 1958 and was opened to traffic on August 12, 1961. Tolls were set in 1962 at $1.30 for car and driver, and $.30 for each passenger. In 1974, tolls were set at a flat $1.50 per car and remained at that level until the bridge sank during a really bad storm. When the bridge reopened in October 1982, tolls were set at $2.50. Tolls were reduced to $2.00 in April 1983. Tolls were *removed* on August 29, 1985. *Removed*."

"Wow, Clark Bar."

"Well, it's true. Conny's right. This tollway bullshit is awful. In Washington state, those guys built a pontoon floating bridge over a saltwater tidal basin that was part of their main highway system, had it sink during a really bad storm, rebuilt the whole damn thing, and had it paid off all in a span of like 25 years. Tolls *removed*. You're telling me we can't figure out how to maintain your basic highway over some of the flattest earth in the whole damn world without using tolls? Come the hell on."

"I'm convinced a guy could run for governor of Illinois based solely on his promise to remove the tollway and win, hands down. Like, 'The only thing I intend to do over my four years as governor is remove the tollway system and the Highway of Illinois State Toll Authority.'"

The zing in Conny's cranium was like fission.

"Blurry, if you lose to Buck, you have to organize Carlsburgians For A Healthy Pentwater."

"Hmmh. Let me guess ..."

"Right. You'll organize a spring clean-up of the Pentwater River in correlation with Earth Day, taking your son's Cub Scout den to do so."

"Conny ..."

"Sweet, if you lose to me, you have to be a host family for a Taiwanese exchange student."

"Fine."

"A male Taiwanese exchange student."

"Oh now what the fuck is that."

"Buck, if you lose to Sweet, you have to learn how to play jazz keyboard."

"Conny ..."

"You can't do this to us."

"If I lose to Buck, I have to learn how to play jazz guitar."

"Christ with a lob-wedge!"

"Conny ..."

"A jazz band."

"Do you guys have any idea the soothing, meditative effect making music can have?"

"What makes you think we need to be soothed?"

"Sure it's soothing. Just ask Jim Morrison."

"Or Ketih Moon."

"Janis Joplin."

"Cobain."

"Alright."

"Bon Scott was soothed."

"Hendrix."

"John Bonham."

"Coltrane."

"Andy Gibb."

"Karen Carpenter."

"They were soothed."

"Sid Vicious."

"Alright."

"You know, George Gershwin died of a head tumor at a relatively young age."

"Something tells me if we organized our own jazz band, given what I know about our, you know, personalities, we probably wouldn't have to worry about experiencing the intensities of say a George Gershwin or a Karen Carpenter."

"Conny …"

The Calm Before The Storm had proven to be just that. There were no thoughts of The Storm, just The Calm. Drives, approach shots, chips, and putts all came with almost effortless efficiency. Pars were made by each man on each hole. No blood. ("No blood" the term used when neither team nor individual has garnered any profit.)

This hole's handicap was set at 14 supposedly as a result of its shortish length and downwind direction. There was, however, no acquiescence made for the amount of accuracy required off the tee here as it is no-kidding frightening to the average golfer. This usually sets off heated discussions about how handicaps are established on certain holes and by whom, and what sobriety level should be required to hold such authority.

—*Chicago Golf*

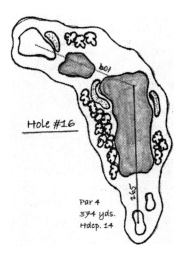

Hole #16

Par 4
374 yds.
Hdcp. 14

Golf is so steeped in etiquette, it can be difficult to differentiate between what is conventional decorum and what are the actual rules of golf. Etiquette is unique to golf because it is an unspoken code of ethics, not a written one, whereas other sports only have rules and aggression. In golf, players say things like "care to play through" and "nice shot" and "man, what a beautiful day" and opponents wish each other well, which can actually be heartfelt a lot of the time because a golfer playing well has an infectious way of boosting other golfers' levels of play. It's kind of a catch-22 that way sometimes. But golfers tend to do what's best for their own game, even if that includes hoping that other golfers play well.

Never step in another player's line when on the green.

Rake sand traps after playing from them.

Do not move or make noise while another player is addressing his ball.

When under a tree, do not break twigs or branches with your practice swing(s).

The player with the best score on the previous hole is first to tee off, then the next players tee off in order of score on that previous hole.

Make as little noise as possible in general.

After teeing off, the player that is furthest away from the hole is next to play until the hole is completed.

Make a mark on your ball so it cannot be mistaken.

Don't make any noise.

Wish a player well before teeing off the 1st tee.

Carry whatever number of clubs you so choose, up to 14.

Never stand directly behind another player while they're hitting and in fact find a place out of their vision to stand, and don't move and be quiet while standing there.

Understand the term "ready" golf and how it is correctly employed.

Conduct yourself appropriately.

Shut up.

Replace divots.

Which of these are rules, and which are characteristic etiquette? Golf is a game so steeped in etiquette, they're almost one and the same. But the real beauty? The real beauty lies in how a blurred "force" between etiquette and rules can be used to really fuck with an opponent at a strategic juncture.

Example of how a blurred "force" between etiquette and rules can be used to really fuck with an opponent at a strategic juncture:

First, keep in mind that "ready" golf is, simply put, hitting when ready. The rules of golf and golf etiquette prescribe the proper way to determine hitting order on a golf course. But "ready" golf allows golfers within a group to hit their shots when ready, even if out of order. Ready golf is a good way to speed up play or at least keep pace. While a lot of golf's subtleties can get lost this way, a keen understanding of ready golf has become tantamount to the Sat. morning foursome maintaining a 4 hr. 15 min. round in the midst of the population explosion. Good etiquette also prescribes that the entire foursome agrees to employ ready golf before anyone in the foursome actually begins employing it. Otherwise, someone could wind up looking like a real asshole.

That being said, one time about 3 years ago, O'Royerson was embroiled in a real pot-boiler with Conny, just the two of them playing a Skins game on a Wed. afternoon. (In a "Skins" game, each hole is given a pre-determined value or "skin." $1 a hole is standard, and would be referred to as a "dollar Skins game." The object is to get the best score on a hole in order to win the skin, compiling as many skins/holes as possible. This is a game where normally presses are not allowed since that sort of negates the pre-determined aspect of the wager, but presses are often too fun for certain personalities to exclude. "Carryovers" generate the tue interest level of a Skins game, carryovers being where two or more players tied for the lowest score on the hole and so the value of the hole was carried over and added to the value of the next hole and is done so in succession until a hole is won outright by a single player. Carryovers oftentimes mean large sums of money can be won on just one hole.) Buck and Conny had customized their particular Skins game that day, as they are want to do, so that it included but was not necessarily limited to: 1) birdies paying double the total value of the hole (carry-overs *included*), 2) eagles paid quadruple, 3) unlimited presses, and 4) a player was not required to be down in order to press. Quite a stretch from the traditional Skins game, one might say. After hitting their approaches on the 14th hole, which O'Royerson pressed since he will par it until the cows come home, Buck was on the green in regulation about 25 ft. from the cup and Conny was also on the green about 3 ft. directly behind Buck about 28 ft. from the cup. As they made their way towards the green that day, Conny experienced a number of delays that began with a need to take a piss from a fresh Old Style. Then, coming out of his piss bush, the strap on his bag gave way kind of mysteriously given that his bag was fairly new at that time. The bag then upended and dumped many of Conny's clubs, some golf balls fell out of a pocket, then other things ensued from that awk-wardness, like Conny hurting his groin when the bag upended again into him right there, and add to that Conny's shoelace becoming untied. All of which not only put Conny well behind Buck in getting to the green, but also caused Conny to be out of breath and pissed off upon approaching the green. Just generally unprepared. This would have been an instance where Buck could have employed ready golf; he would have had plenty of time read his putt thoroughly and putt out both in the interest of pace of play and so that Conny wouldn't feel pressured to hurry his putt. Technically, however, Buck's putting out before Conny got to the green would mean he played out of turn, and to be fair, when there's money on the line via a home-made Skins game, it's probably prudent to follow the rules. Buck decided to wait for Conny. See, Buck was going to be able to go to school on Conny's putt, enhancing Buck's chances of winning what were 24 skins after a fourth press by the time they reached the 14th hole, where Buck had a putt for birdie (24 = 48) on a hole which he essentially owns. Also, Conny would never have enough time to calm down from his Jerry Lewis impersonation back there to gather himself enough to putt well; there was a group behind him and Buck. Chances are, Buck knew this. So Buck waited for Conny to putt first. Conny naturally 3-putted for bogey, gave Buck a real good idea on the line of his birdie putt, Buck sinking the 25-footer with a whoomp and a fist pump and a claim that "48" wasn't just the number of lower contintental United States anymore as if that was the only possible application for that particular number. Buck had adhered to the rules of golf *and* its code of etiquette, and he was able to utilize a sometimes blurred force between etiquette and rules in order to fuck Conny over.

The one par-3 respite during Dog-Leg Run, the tee box here at The Bone is somewhat elevated with the wind usually kicking in from behind. Given the length golfers have trekked to this point, and given the fact that the only other par-3 in the last 9 holes is "Jason" the 13th, golfers, many of them battered by now, have been seen licking actual wounds here.

—*Chicago Golf*

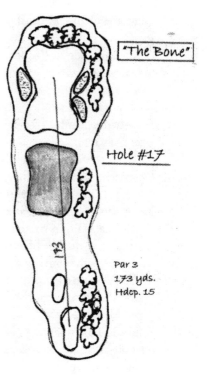

"The Bone"

Hole #17

173

Par 3
173 yds.
Hdcp. 15

The walk from the 6th green to the tee of The Storm is a tightrope. Anuses do clench. Conny was -1 par, and he has stood on the tee of The Storm at -1 before, actually. He has no good memories to fall back on here though. Only severe losses. And guys were all still well within striking distance should Conny implode here again. Buck was +1, Blurry +2, and Sweet, who had battled back admirably after double bogey at the 1st hole's Noose, which isn't like Sweet at all, was at +3. They each saw The Storm as their chance to wipe the slate clean. If the front-9 was over and done with at this point, Sweet and his famished 7-handicap would be 1) knee deep in the Pentwater

River with the honors biology class from Carlsburg High planting water lilies around Girl Scout Island, the honors class knowing the reason why more than Sweet perhaps, 2) preparing materials for a presentation on how we as humans can consume—and by that he means not only digest, but purchase—immediately biodegradable materials only, and 3) offering several teens just released from juvenile detention for B&Es and their parents advice on how to correct the situation based on what parents did between 1915-1925, Sweet's credentials for doing so as a 40-year old man in 2003 being highly questionable; Blurry would be 1) contacting Habitat for Humanity on where to sign up as laborer and financier, and 2) researching the dietary and exercise regimens of American pioneers as they relate to his new back-to-basics program called Physio-'Neers; Buck would be 1) preparing his campaign for city council and wondering what it would be like to be the only man serving there, minus Nate Cash, and also wondering if any of the ladies on city council like to get high; and Conny would be scot-free. The numbers and range of emotions running through Conny's head at that point are what climaxes in movies about tortured artists' lives are made of. He had gone from neutral to manic to void, all in the walk from the 6th green to the 7th tee.

The landscape of the golf course changes dramatically here, Triple-the-Pines emerging from its pines and oaks to confront 1831 Marsh head on. The 7th hole faces *and* runs alongside the wetland as it has two sets of men's tee boxes. One plays from app. 190 yds. but does not have to carry 1831 Marsh as much as it just needs to avoid it to the right; the other tee box is about 25 yds. southwest and plays from app. 170 yds. alongside the marsh, having to carry a good portion of the marsh that juts in, to the point that the green is semi-islandish with water front/right/back, but safe land on the left side. What the longer tee box avoids in water hazard it more than makes up for in wind hazard. And while the shorter-distance tee box is shorter and not angled into the wind, it can harbor a brutal crosswind at times. Again, anuses do clench.

Marti Lynn Morley's appearance on the 7th tee could not have been timed any better. Her beverage cart hydroplaned briefly on creamy aurae.

"Please mum, may I have some More-ly." Buck cupped his hands and Marti Lynn put a jumbo Old Style in them like into a basket.

"You boys are beautiful, you know that? I really mean it. Out here walking 5 miles on such a gorgeous day. I think it's great."

Buck popped the cap the way most people unconsciously scratch. "And great it is."

They all stood there around the beverage cart, Conny, Buck, Blurry, Sweet, and Marti Lynn, and they felt themselves being a group alone out on the edge of 1831 Marsh then, a feeling that did not come with a weight so much as a click. Jarring at first then incredibly comfortable.

"Old Styles all around?"

"Who could ask for More-ly?"

The curiosity was burning holes in plural recesses of Marti Lynn's cranium. And it was directly affecting her peony.

"So, what's the game today? It can't be Closest To The Rough or whatever that game was. You're moving too good."

The guys frothed with competitive zest. Their eagerness and attentiveness could not be masked. They glimmered in a private sun of pacts, and rippled. Their human bodies were glimmering and rippling, then smoothing, then rippling, then glimmering.

"Just the usual Scotch game with a Nassau."

Marti Lynn's considerable bosom settled and she put money in her pouch. "Yeah well, you're certainly going all out on it today."

Guys were surprised to hear that it was written on their face. Marti Lynn wished them well and drove off. She became a white canopied dot parachuting down into a multi-green world.

Buck, Blurry, and Sweet each secretly felt that the 7th hole Storm was probably the best chance for the Nassau to get evened up. It was known as a trouble hole for Conny. Even so, Sweet and Blurry looked at each other and shook their heads "no" to the idea of pressing Force 2, their faces still pinkish possibly from the scarlet embarrassment that tactic produced on the 4th hole. They were probably biding their time as best they could over the 7th and 8th holes, knowing that Blurry would be the only one to get a stroke at the 9th hole, which Blurry can score well on a fair amount of the time as The Duck Blind suits his gift for course management, that gift having become a down-right bounty in the absence of a cell phone. A good time to press again if necessary, the 9th hole, especially since Blurry gets a stroke *again* on the 10th hole, not a bad little buffer at all, and the only place on the course where that will happen for Sweet and Blurry during the Scotch game. For the first time since The Noose, Conny felt like he didn't have any advantage whatsoever over his opponents, as if there was no score yet, only even ground, so much could happen here at The Storm. Conny had honors, and he would be the anally clenched guinea pig by which all others took measure.

The tee box that day was the furthest one. The yardage iden-tification process here was identical to the par-3 4th hole. Blurry found the sprinklerhead with yardage on it (184) near the front of the tee box and walked off yardage to the blue tees (184 + 12 = 196). Sweet stood at the front of the tee box and threw up grass, though it actually meant something here since there was a bit of wind now coming over 1831 Marsh. Conny paced the yardage off for himself. Buck drank beer and asked Conny.

"That pin looks dead center. Slight breeze at us. I'm playing it 200 even to the pin."

But yardage was the least of their problems. Aside from some of the gnarliest penal gorse-like rough on the course being set free to rule the greenside by Phil Black, the truly dastardly part of the 7th hole is its perspective from the tee box. Hand-held by the north woods to look over the secretive marsh and further to the western sky, the large northern Illinois sky starting from endlessness above then coming down to valance the marsh, the view so intriguing—catch it during twilight with the wife and marriage-saving copulation is sure to ensue, often right then and there—that even though guys know they must battle hard here, the wonder of it all is too distracting, as are the memories of outdoor copulation.

There was nowhere for Conny to turn to for soothing neutrality here. Everywhere he looked, there was inspiration and awareness and goals to pursue, including: preserving -1; not losing ground in the freakish Nassau; losing ground in the freakish Nassau; beating Sweet and Blurry bloody for money; again, preserving -1; *breaking 75*. For someone who was -1, Conny sure was a mess.

Conny's tee shot on 7: Here's a good example of what golf is like: Conny is embroiled in a mind-bending, friendship-endangering bet, and with three men not too lacking in the cut-throat department. None of them wants to lose (maybe Conny does in a strange way, but not really), and each has his own signature head-fuck that he will try to employ at strategic junctures, except under one condition—when somebody has a special, life-affirming round going. Conny was teeing his ball up on the 7th hole and he was -1, and Buck, Blurry, and Sweet sincerely hoped to see Conny do well here, to see a round under par in-person, to see it here at Triple-the-Pines. But Conny's coming completely undone wouldn't "exactly be piss in our oatmeal either" Sweet sort of mumbled to the marsh. Golf is like *that*. Conny was pumped, adrenaline-fueled. The slight breeze into him would allow Conny to pull 5-iron and take a comfortable full swing with it. While his club selection was very comfortable, Conny's head was not. With his neutrality depleted now, he took the club back feeling absolutely no feeling in his hands, arms, shoulders, or cranium and with a weird kind of clamp on his stamen, and he really just hoped for the best. This is a bad way to set up over a ball on a long par-3 with nothing but water and highly punitive gorse-like rough around it, no two ways about it. By the time Conny was at the top of his swing, he just wanted to make contact, to avoid topping it or chunking it, or missing it completely, a thought that did pop into his head. Well, that's just not going to get the job done that kind of mind frame won't, and Conny's ball wound up starting left and then hooking more left, a ridiculously obvious guard against the marsh and an indicator of both his lack of feel in certain areas and the overfelt clamp in others, and Conny's ball landed in penal gorse-like rough some 25 yds. left and short of the green where upon impact it did not resurface, Conny hoping to be able to just find the damn thing. Buck, Blurry, and Sweet were disappointed and elated then, but with maybe a good solid bent towards elation.

"Ahh, it's a tough shot, Con-stance."

"It's daunting."

Around the 7th green, voices rang out as balls were discovered. Conny continued to search a wide area well left of the green. It's important to note that a lost ball in a wide-open area that is in-bounds is the worst fate one shot can possibly endure in golf, bar none. A ball in a water hazard or out-of-bounds comes with an answer at least. Fair enough. But a lost ball in a wide-open area that is in-bounds is unbearable. The golfer knows it's there, "you can't tell me it's not," etc. It is the lack of closure, the lost asset, the resulting penalty, but mostly it is the injustice. The most dangerous result of the lost ball in a wide-open area that is in-bounds is its demoralization. It is discouraging. How does one rationalize such a fate, and why would one try to go on if this is their fate? I.e., What's in the hell is the point? If golf was not so strange, one might stop right then and there from its mistreatment, but golf is so strange that one must find out what could possibly be next. That's all well and good until one remembers that the penalty for a lost ball is stroke and distance. The rule book, should anybody ever care to look at it, will tell you "stroke and distance," which makes a player go back to the spot he originally played his ball from and play it again, also counting the stroke he took for his first, lost attempt. In all fairness to the golfing public, this does take a lot of time and is unrealistic to enforce during the population explosion. Hence, it is usually limited to official tournament play. The thing is, with pacts on the line in their creative Nassau, this foursome's impromptu game on Mon., July 28, 2003 had taken on more weight than all the tournaments they had ever entered, combined. The Nassau had become heavy then. Conny started to fear the worst, and with good reason.

Guys came over to Conny's area to help him try to find his ball. As they looked, different approaches to the enforcement of the lost ball rule appeared to Conny, each of which have been used by these guys at one time or another, including: 1) the guys could agree to have Conny just drop a ball in the area where they were searching for his lost ball and say "we know it's here somewhere, just drop one, no penalty," or 2) guys could sort of look at each other and wait for Conny's good nature to oblige itself to the importance of this particular Nassau this particular day and walk back to the tee box to play his next shot, which would be the correct enforcement of the lost ball rule in this case. As they looked around for another 3-4 minutes, Conny glanced back to see how far behind them Tommy Sheehan's following group was, and would it afford him time to walk back to the tee to play his next shot. He did not see Tommy's twirling club.

The walk back during a correct enforcement of the lost ball rule does make you want to quit, no matter who you are. Guys waited for Buck to say something to Conny.

"What do you want to do, Bro?"

"That thing's probably buried underground." Conny kept kicking gorse-like rough around. He really didn't want to make that walk.

"Could be."

"However you want to play it, Con-stance."

"That sucks, Con-dola."

"Yeah. I guess I better walk it back to the tee."

"I don't think we'll be slowing anybody up if you do."

"I better play it that way today then." He really didn't want to go.

"Might actually be better than playing it from Satan's Tossed Salad here."

"Yeah. Guess that's what I'll do then. I'll walk it back."

The walk back to the 7th tee box gave Conny time to think, which was the last thing he wanted. Not thinking had been working so well; now this. As Conny made his way over the 190 yds. of the slight incline back to the tee box, Marti Lynn Morley spied on him and the guys while she waited under a pine tree for Tommy Sheehan's group to approach the 6th green, hopefully thirsty. She saw Conny trudging his way back to the tee, so completely bereft that his head actually hung. Conny was in such turmoil that he forgot to just take one or two clubs back with him to the tee; instead he carried his whole bag like he had just pulled it from a foxhole. It looked like someone had dumped limestone in it.

"Good lord." The curiosity in Marti Lynn's cranium actually bubbled.

Buck and Sweet and Blurry made their bogies on The Storm, not bad, so they were on Conny's heels with two holes to go on the front-9. The breeze from the northwest picked up just a knot, making 1831 Marsh the prevalent atmosphere. Though the 8th hole's tee box does technically contend with 1831 Marsh at its front, the 7th hole is the only hole on the front-9 that brings the marsh so directly into play. Yet Conny felt like he had been up against the wetland for like the last hour. Buck, being a real friend to Conny and understanding the sting that came not just from triple-bogey but also from the fact that Conny was now tied with Buck in the outlandish Nassau, made an attempt at levity during practice swings on the 8th tee box.

"You know Conny, there are a lot of vague terms around these pacts. 'Campaign for' and 'develop' and 'write an article series.' What do they really mean?"

"'Try.'"

"I see. 'Try.'"

"Yeah."

"That sounds great, Conny, but, um, I guess what I mean is how are we supposed to go about trying? You say you're going to campaign for the elimination, and you mean total elimination, of the State Illinois Toll Highway Authority. How do you 'campaign' for that, I guess is what I mean."

"I see we're suddenly focusing on what if I should lose. I would think you might be a little more concerned about having to run for city council, my friend."

"Well, at least that 'campaign' would be a bit more well defined, now wouldn't it?"

Buck was teeing up his ball and realizing he had made a poor choice in his attempt at levity.

"Would it? Have you seen these guys on the campaign 'trail'? What is their intent, exactly?"

"Yeah, but at least they tell you exactly how they're going to do it."

"What?"

"Come on, Conny. I mean, at least they're very plain in how they would go about fixing things—they'll take office."

"None of those guys have ever cited a specific problem and their specific solution for that problem. Ever. Have they ever cited a very specific problem and their plan for solving it? At least I have a very specific problem, specific problems, that I intend to solve."

"OK, but how Conny? You've got the specific problem; Nate Cash, for example, has the specific office. How about you get together with Nate."

"How about you take Nate's seat in office and we do it together, Buck."

"Delusional. Totally delusional."

Guys settled as Buck addressed his tee ball. Motivated by the closing gap on the Nassau, he laced a beauty dead center, 265 yds.

"Nice, Bucko."

"You guys do realize that a Carlsburg city councilman has absolutely no influence on the Illinois State Highway Toll Authority, right?"

"It's the principle, Clark Bar."

"Oh."

"OK, so who would have the influence necessary to bring down the tollway, Bro-mide?" It was as though Buck was canvassing now. He rested his chin in the crotch of his thumb and forefinger.

"People living in the counties where the tollway is housed refuse to use the tollway for one day, also refusing to go to work that day. Have you any idea the loss of revenue?"

"Conny ..."

"There's only one thing these people understand, and that's revenue generation."

"Conny's right."

"Steve Forbes had a very specific answer to a very specific problem. People bitch and moan and bitch and moan and bitch and moan about taxes, this guy comes along and says '17% flat tax,' and all it does it seem to scare the shit out of everybody."

"I was in love with Steve Forbes."

"I never resented his wealth or upbringing, or both."

Blurry teed his ball up, loose as a goose, took a few practice swings without a damn thing on his mind, stepped up with driver and almost made 100% connection with it, sending the ball up the right side of the fairway about 250 yds.

"That works, Tom."

"I always thought it was kind of weird that we have this massive tollway system and we have possibly the worst roads in the entire country. I don't get that. Not at all."

"Gee, I wonder where the money could be going." Conny's sarcasm never meant to make other people feel stupid, but they did anyway sometimes. He was alluding to graft and corruption.

"Did I tell you guys about when I was out in Washington state?"

"I'm not even going to get into the ridiculously corruptive nature of basically every industry associated with transportation in Chicagoland. The point is, the tollway has been ruining the quality of life here unnecessarily for too long, and it has got to go, no pun intended."

"I agree with Conny."

"I'm saying how, Conny."

"17% flat tax rate is all the guy said. 'Cross the board. People ran for the freaking hills. We had our chance."

Sweet might have been the most buoyed by his bogey on the 7th hole, having played the hole best out of the group but just missing on a 5-footer for par. Clark Bar felt his game turning around and his tee shot on the 8th reflected his newfound confidence, charging one right up the middle almost side-by-side with Buck.

"Clarkie. Nice."

"Bottom line? We get 5 million people in Chicagoland together for one day. If we can convince 5 million people that they can get whatever they want by not going to work for a day, maybe two, we're there."

"Conny …"

"So, basically, your saying 'strike,' is what your saying."

"For a day. Yeah."

"Not to play devil's advocate or anything here Bro, but OK, how do you do *that*?"

"Don't you ever wonder how Steve Forbes never even had a *chance*?"

Conny teed his ball up and took practice swings looking like a man trying to find his game at that point. After his agony during The Storm, and with Buck, Blurry, and Sweet all in great shape off the 8th tee, Conny was experiencing one of the competitive emotions unique to golf—playing catch-up while still in the lead. He had lost momentum, and in disastrous fashion. In extremely embarrassing fashion. After six holes of pure-grade brilliance, one hole had evened the score with Buck and brought Sweet and Blurry back to life. The dynamics of the Nassau were changing rapidly, and front-9 pacts were becoming real to Conny with the equal rush that they were becoming avoidable to Buck, Blurry, and Sweet. He put everything behind him and took the torque-minded swing that had been his since he was 17 years old and the ball shot out of the tee box. Though it tailed on him just enough to reach the rough on the right side, he had made excellent contact and would have a wide-open shot to the green. Conny craved indifferent neutrality, but all he could feel was hope.

Walking the 8th hole comes with the same emotional poke as when you're nearing home when you're ready to be home. You leave 1831 Marsh behind for the time being, and all it comes with, and begin to peek around to see the very scorable 9th hole and right behind that the modest clubhouse waiting for its chance to give you a break and a beer. Guys got off the tee well here, a must on this hole in order to score, and they were able to relax on their walk. Conny noticed that Tommy Sheehan's group had caught up to them, they were no longer two holes behind, a dagger of a reminder of Conny's extended time spent on The Storm. Sweet sidled up to Conny.

"Con-stantly Brooding Bro-mide."

"That damn hole, man."

"Put it behind you, mon frere."

"You played it well, Clark Bar."

"I agree with you."

"Your game's coming around, Clarkie. Some nice shots on this front-9."

Sweet sidled closer. "How about a charity golf tournament, with the proceeds going towards a camping trip for pre-teens to Puget Sound?"

"That's in Washington state, right?"

"Indeed."

"A charity golf tournament."

"Yeah. Proceeds go to a camping trip for pre-teens to Puget Sound, chaperoned of course by someone familiar with the area."

"It kind of smacks of an all-expenses paid vacation, Clarkie."

"Nothing with anything over two pre-teens is a vacation. This would be for 10-12 kids and two chaperones."

"Chaperones aren't allowed to drink. Did you know that?"

"I just think it's a good idea to show kids something like Puget Sound before they begin to form too many opinions about things, and before Puget Sound starts harboring Burger Kings. Yeah."

"Hmmh. OK. You lose to Blurry on the back-9, and it's yours."

Walking into the 8th fairway offers a broad view of Triple-the-Pines. The 8th and 9th holes dissect Triple-the-Pines going west to east back towards the clubhouse; the 10th and 11th holes dissect the course going east to west back to 1831 Marsh; the front-9 is on the north side and the back-9 is on the south side; North Pond is on the south side of the 10th hole; all of it in view from the middle of the 8th fairway. Conny took one more look over at Tommy Sheehan's group behind him to see how well they were keeping pace.

"OK gentlemen, let me sum up pacts for the back-9 if I may."

"Oh wow."

"Cool."

Guys were feeling too good to be comprehended. Perfect weather, beer in hand (and early, which was fun sometimes), walking the 8th fairway to their tee shots, the world in front of them, and not unreasonable chances to break 40 on the front-9 at Triple-the-Pines.

"Sweet, if you lose to Blurry on the back-9, you have to organize a charity golf tournament to raise funds for a trip for pre-teens to Puget Sound for a camping trip."

"OK! Whatever!" Sweet was great, but he was also way too transparent at this point. A third beer and subsequently wilder hand gesticulation had made his attempt at a private meeting with Conny a bit obvious, as did Conny with his own third beer choosing that particular pact less than a minute after it had been devised. There were just too many self-rewarding things associated with this pact, so Buck and Blurry raised hell about it.

"Wait a minute, I'm not done yet, ladies. Buck, if you lose to Blurry, you have to organize a charity golf tournament to raise money for the ju-co scholarship."

"It's no trip to Puget Sound."

"Maybe Clark Bar should have to take some of the troubled teens that he will somehow become an expert on parenting, WWII-generation style."

"Yeah, I wanna wake up in some ancient forest with a camping knife in my head."

"Blurry, if you lose to me, you have to organize a charity golf tournament to raise money for the Everybody House."

"Sorry?"

"The Everybody House. The Col. Erasmus A. Bettinger Pentwater Valley House for Transitioning Families. Commonly known as The Everybody House."

"Transitioning families."

"Right."

"There's a charity for helping people move?"

Buck looked away, frozen.

"Transitioning means families who have hit hard times and need a place to stay, but are working on pulling themselves up again, like tangibly."

"Transitioning means that?"

"If I lose to Sweet, I have to organize a charity golf tournament to raise money for a trip for pre-teens to the Florida Keys for a snorkeling trip."

"No way, pal."

"Conny …"

As they made their way up the fairway to their approach shots, Conny reminded Buck and Blurry, several times in fact, that while, yes, his and Sweet's charity golf tournaments would result in trips to remote and exotic destinations, they would also have 10-15 pre-teens in tow, possibly some who have committed B&Es, whereas Buck and Blurry would be completely done with their charity tournament duties pretty much by the time they walked off the 18th hole, simply presenting a check to their charities at a later date. It made sense, and each man settled around his ball to get down to the business of an approach shot, Conny walking up ahead on the right to see what kind of lie he had.

Patterns of inebriation had not made themselves too readily apparent at this point, but they were lurking; Blurry chose a club from his bag and addressed his ball, then realized he had pulled his sandwedge though he stood approximately 172 yds. from the pin, for example. It was quickly recognized and rectified, and you don't *have* to be inebriated to make such a false start, but inebriation did lurk in this case.

Buck sidled up to Conny.

"So how's work been going, Con-stance?"

"Busy as ever."

"Yeah."

"You?"

"Way too much work right now."

"Yeah."

"This market just doesn't have any let-up. It's crazy. How are things at home?"

Conny sized up Buck's face.

"I'm just asking."

"They're fine, Bucko. You?"

"Same as it ever was."

"Sorry to hear it."

"So, um, what's up with these pacts then?"

"What do you mean so what's up with these pacts then? Have I been unclear in explaining them? See, if you lose to Clark Bar on the front-9 …"

"Fine, fine, fine."

"Are you not sick of treading the same old ground sometimes, Bucko? That's what's up with these pacts so then. Don't you ever get the feeling that we're taking the wrong approach, pretty much day in and day out? Like worse than just 'backwards'? Possibly wasting some incredibly valuable time?"

"All the time."

"Don't you ever want to do something about it?"

"No."

"I'm serious."

"So am I. Look, I work hard, I play hard, I take care of my family and I've never killed anyone."

"That's quite the vitae, Buck."

"I do my best not to be an asshole to people and when I am I try to make it up to them, and that's really all I ask in return."

"This seems to cover it for you, does it?"

"Most of the time it really does. Have you taken the time to consider the success of having never killed anyone?"

"Oh, brother. So, where does the participation come in? Nay, the fun."

"I work hard, I play hard, I take care of my family and I've never killed anyone. I do my best not to be an asshole to people and when I am I try to make it up to them."

"Buck, you're not getting out of any obligations today, if that's what this is about."

"That's not my concern at all. Have I ever welched? I agreed to the bet, I'll live up to it. Hell, I'm in pretty good shape right now as far as that all goes what with being tied for the lead and all, eh? You're not getting out of any obligations either, you know. I just thought I'd check to see if everything's OK."

"Man, ask a guy to run for city council and suddenly you're Jeffrey Dahmer."

"It's not that you just asked anyone to run for city council. You asked *me*. This indicates a machine imbalance to me, Conny. I wonder if your load is lop-sided, so to speak."

"I say worry about your own damn load."

"Just thought I'd check."

Their approach shots did not take advantage of their quality drives. Guys were laid out all around the 8th green and dispensed themselves accordingly as they approached that area. The first to play in this situation, Sweet stood solidly over his chip shot, with excellent balance but also *relaxed*. With his back to the rest of the guys and his oddly perfect ass setting off the imperfections of the rest of him, Sweet opened up the face of his sandwedge, kept his head very still, took a short but quick and forceful back-and-through swing, and the ball popped up into the air to land softly about 8 ft. in front of the hole, dead on line, coming to rest about 2 ft. away. Sweet simply grabbed the putter from his bag and went up and tapped in his par putt without really thinking twice about it before Buck, Conny, or Blurry had a chance to play their next shots, not that they were ready to after seeing that. Seeing Sweet make par so matter of factly, remaining guys each hit mediocre shots from around the green and subsequently bogeyed the hole. They had been put off. Not due to any lack of respect or etiquette at all on Clark Bar's part. He was nowhere in the wrong for playing ready golf the way he did. That is to say, it was not Clark Bar that repelled or annoyed the other guys, it was his newfound confidence that did it. Confidence, *which a 7-handicapper should have, right?*, Sweet took immense pleasure in telepathically transmitting to Buck, Conny, and Blurry.

Sweet's par incited actual queasiness in Conny. For all his earnestness, it was incredibly frustrating that pacts were not just rolling off the tip of his tongue, that he didn't have them all at the ready in fact. As they made their way to the 9th tee box, Conny became acutely aware of his queasiness, and was able to note to himself that it had one major effect over two distinct areas the queasiness did, that one effect being a dissonance, the two areas being:

1) neutrality and
2) hope.

A double dog-leg, this sprawling 568-yd. par-5 snakes its way from the southernmost forest through more oak-lined fairway to the double-tiered green hugging North Pond on its left side. And yes, the hole is shaped somewhat like a jack-knife, but—locals like to remind—let's not forget that's also the term often used when describing a horrible kind of crash.
—*Chicago Golf*

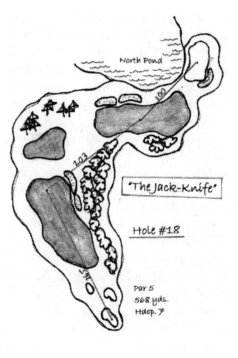

North Pond

"The Jack-Knife"

Hole #18

Par 5
568 yds.
Hdcp. 7

Sweet, on the other hand, was absolutely on fire. With one hole left on the front-9, he was tied with Blurry and one stroke down to Conny and Buck. Buck was preoccupied, one might say, with the euphoria of the addict, knowing Sweet and Blurry would press again here (1 = 2 = 4 points) plus the fact that he could very well be running for city council, which was worth more than actual money, Christ almighty. And with the 9th hole being a par-5, anything could happen. Buck's arms and chest and cranium were fizzing and he couldn't quite feel his legs then, which felt great to him.

Blurry was having a hard time going into cahoots with his partner in order to gain a few dollars in the Scotch game when knowing full well that the 7-handicapper has indeed hit his stride and, with one shot, could force Blurry into recycling other people's shit for a year. As they took the 9th tee box, Blurry congratulated Sweet on his nice par on the 8th hole and they nodded "yes" to each other to pressing Force 2, and Blurry felt a little sick from doing both. Their press was accepted by Force 2 From Namino, WI That Is.

With points being 1 = 4 now, dollar a point, guys calculated out loud what an *umbrella* would garner, that being 4 (original) = 8 (umbrella) = 16 (first press) = 32 (second press). And while these bumped-up numbers were not without their weight, guys had finally and at last come to the decision that $32 meant nothing compared to some of their impending obligations.

Sweet's tee shot on 9: Beaming, like tangibly, from his recent stellar play and its subsequent shift in momentum, and being kind of insufferable, Clark Bar stepped up to his ball with confidence, stood over it squarely with excellent posture, and took possibly the best swing he had taken up to that point that day. Buck wondered if Sweet's ass had ever looked more perfect, as a thing. His ball took a perfectly straight line down the center of the fairway, probably about 265 yds., and it added something like another *layer* to Sweet's insufferability.

"Beauty, Clark Bar."

"Garden spot."

"Some troubled teens are really gonna miss out on one helluva mentor."

Buck's tee shot on 9: His mind scrambling to do the math, Buck had used the time during Sweet's tee shot to try to actually get math out of his head, to approach his own tee shot with a clear if not downright empty head, an empty head being most conducive to some of Buck's best golf shots. But the euphoria of the addict was definitely sinking in. The thing about the euphoria is, though most people tend to equate "euphoria" with something "good," it isn't always a good thing as far as Buck's golf game is concerned. Euphoria feels great to Buck, but it does not necessarily help him make well-balanced golf swings. Euphoria has a tendency to make Buck waver, for example. Nonetheless, Blurry and Sweet had pressed for a second time, pacts were coming to a head, and the foursome were in a real horserace with no man being more that one stroke up/down. So, if you're Buck, you're going to have euphoria. In this particular instance, the wavering caused him to pull-hook his drive into the pines down the left side of the hole, where they echoed Buck's failure.

"You might have a shot out of there. It's happened before."

"I think I saw where it ended up, Bucko. Got an eye on it."

Where the absence of Blurry's cell phone had promoted total clarity—total clarity for the entire foursome at certain points—its lack of distraction had now become a distraction. Basically, *where the hell was it?* What other guys could not know was that Blurry himself had been tiring of the cell phone for some time. There's simply no way guys could have known that. Not a single indicator of that at all, ever. The other thing guys could not have known about was:

> About a week prior to July 28, 2003, Blurry had decided to take the train into the office and wound up being seated directly behind another businessman and on the other side of the aisle were some college students. The businessman was on a two-way walkie-talkie radio "phone." The college students were the Bohemian kind, possibly grad students. It didn't take any time at all—the train had not started moving yet—for the college students to make it apparent that they saw the businessman on the two-way radio phone while on a train as being what's wrong with the world today. They did this via an assortment of condescending glares and hand-muffled

comments while glaring. Initially, Blurry took heart in seeing that things on campus were still the-establishment-as-devil, as well they should be, he thought, seeing as how this will be the only time in their lives that they can view the establishment as devilish if they ever intend to, say, take out a mortgage loan later on, for example. The businessman was on his walkie-talkie phone when his traditional-style cell phone rang from one of his pockets. There was something about the way he answered it to his other free ear as though he was completely isolated from the rest of the train that Blurry found off-putting as he had been finding this kind of single to double radio-cellular scenario in public places off-putting for a while now, and the Bohemian college students found it disgusting. Blurry thought the students may have actually had a bit of fear mixed in with their looks of disgust too. The college students did not hide their jeering looks from the businessman, which, brave as that may seem, wasn't really much of a feat considering he was in his own world via telephony and never even knew they were there. He never knew they were there as he got off the walkie-talkie and held his cell phone conversation on the train for the next 30 min. Afterwhich, he got off at his stop in Oak Park, IL still talking. Blurry watched him walk the platform and down the stairs phone still to ear and occasionally saying something back into the walkie-talkie phone too, and he looked back Blurry did to the college students to see them shaking their heads in that particular way that people in their early 20s have to convey disdain that is unmistakably *you'll never catch me pulling that shit* or *fuck that noise*. This was still kind of endearing to Blurry in the Bohemian, establishment-as-devil way until the college students started to make fun of the businessman after he had left the train, still on the phone(s) three blocks down the street. That was when Blurry secretly made sure his cell phone was turned off, using the seat in front of him as a barrier. In making fun of the businessman, one of the Bohemians noted the addictive nature of the cell phone, and how its entire success is based on how humans are prey to the kind of peer pressure something as simple as a cell phone can ignite, i.e., *I can't be seen alone in public as though I don't have a constant need for a cell phone to my ear*, or *all my friends have one*, etc., and how having a cell phone to quell the peer pressure ignited from not having one created a truly physical dependence on cell phones. And they had a way of discussing these things in that Bohemian tone of voice that makes them so unattractive that they actually had no choice in their ostracization from the mainstream, so that becoming Bohemian was really decided for them based on their natural tone of voice, not a choice they made for themselves, but thank God they had "Bohemia" to turn to as their club. What might be most annoying about Bohemians, Blurry thought at that moment on the train as he turned his phone off, is that some of the things they say still have a way of hitting home. (It seems Bohemians do get to be a free spirit *and* a public conscience, simultaneously ... but, man, that tone of fucking voice.) Something made Blurry decide to go with the Bohemians on this one, and he began to set new non-cellular goals. One of those goals would be to play Triple-the-Pines without the cell phone on his hip at his first possible chance, and for the first time in close to five years. Blurry would try to kick. This he did Wed. afternoon of that week, shot 79, and waited with secretly bated breath for Conny's next invitation, which came the morning of July 28, 2003.

Blurry's tee shot on 9: The Duck Blind 9th hole sets up to Blurry's eye very nicely, the hole being an exercise in course management. Blurry would need all the advantage he could get here, being really scared at that moment about the pacts that lay in front of him, being one stroke down to Buck and Conny and tied with Sweet, and Sweet being hot. Buck's tee shot into the woods had rekindled Blurry's years-ignored relationship with "optimism." Something as basic as 230 yds. anywhere in the fairway would be all he needed. Catching the ball high on the clubface but with a fair amount of force, his tee shot got high into the air and curled right to left about 210 yds. out, landing in the left rough but with an open second shot. Not ideal, but not in the pine-crapper either like Buck. Relationship with optimism still smoldering.

"OK, Tom."

"That won't hurt you."

Conny was brimming with hope, ambition, and passion.

Conny's tee shot on 9: Conny had been concocting his version of God since he was about 12 years old, and he was now begging that God to help him get rid of his hope, ambition, and passion. *Please, instill in me the indifferent neutrality that made me -1 after 6 holes.* But even though Conny himself had concocted the God, it still seemed to work in mysterious ways seeing as how Conny's begging was only leading to more heightened amounts of hope, ambition, and passion. It also didn't help that he had Led Zeppelin's "Communication Breakdown" pulsating through his cranium, with a resulting twitch over his left eyebrow somehow. That really didn't help at all. As a cure, Conny could only imagine the things he had done correctly in the past. He simply put a picture of a successful drive in his head, that is he jammed it in there with everything else, kept his eye on the ball, and pulled the trigger. The ensuing shot was reflective of Conny himself; it had a little bit of everything going on. The ball felt like it came off the hozel slightly and started to semi-knuckleball it out to the right, but a nervously exaggerated emphasis on follow-through gave the ball a boomerang-like effect, causing the knuckleballer to some-how draw back left. It hooked, really. The ball never got real high in the air. There was a point while it was still flailing just above the ground like that, when it was hooking and knuckleballing, that Conny, in the deepest pit of the area where he is able to be honest with himself, admitted that he was just happy not to have missed the ball completely. It was in that same pit where Conny would come to accpet his 226-yd. drive to the secondary cut of rough down the left side as a monumental success.

The guys were catapulted from the 9th tee box without any chance of hiding their intense motivation to avoid pacts. Spending the last 8 holes playing excellent golf, making some truly great shots and scoring well, all on what was proving to be the most beautiful day in recent memory in Carlsburg, IL; these things were propelling them involuntarily. Add to that the break and a beer that was waiting for them in the clubhouse at the end of this hole, and it was like they were being propelled and pulled at the same time.

"Another could be to campaign for the repeal of the seat belt law."

Conny had twelve pacts left to communicate before the 10th tee, and he needed to make the most use of his time between now and then. His heart was actually pounding.

"Repeal the seat belt law?"

"Yes."

"My guess is we would have to threaten the revenue stream again to achieve that one."

"You got it."

"Of course I'm afraid to ask, but, how?"

Conny's passion was at about fourth-beer-before-noon level. "No one in the state uses their car for a day. All of us on the same day, that is. This includes not going to work. They're so damned concerned about our safety? Call this the ultimate in car safety. And we'll call it that until they repeal the damn law, and we'll do it all from the very comfort of home. Until we get what we want. What we deserve. A nice little byproduct will be the threat to the Illinois Highway Toll State Authority, too. Pretty basic, really."

"You know, maybe we could threaten gas prices with this non-car use while we're at it."

"Have you any idea what we could get back for ourselves if we only threaten not to use our cars, all at the same time, for like a day?"

"I know a guy whose life was saved by using his seat belt."

"That's great. I mean it, it really is. And since everybody who gets into a car knows that's what they're there for, it should then be left up to us to make that choice to buckle up for ourselves. We could pretend that every properly licensed driver is an actual adult, if necessary. If the seat belt law is not the biggest governmental revenue generation scam this side of cigarette taxes and the Illinois Toll Highway State Authority, I'll eat my hat."

"I don't think you can call the cigarette tax a scam, per se. They're not really hiding their intentions on that one. Now, the Illinois Highway Authority State Toll System? Oh, that's a fucking scam. Yeah."

"I never realized we could accomplish so much by not going to work."

"Is there nowhere left where we can make decisions for ourselves? You're telling me it's against the *law* for me not to choose to put my own seat belt on? I mean, the *law*? You can't be serious. To make putting on your seat belt a law mocks both citizenship and the law. It treats us like children."

"It coddles us, in a bad way."

"It induces resentment."

"I agree with Clark Bar."

"The scariest part about it, though, is the way we just roll over like sheep."

"Plus what about those 'seat belt enforcement zones'? How can it be constitutional?"

"I think you mean either we're sheep, or we roll over. Not both."

"Oh, we're both alright. We are sheep, rolling over to take it in the ass. We let these dillwads tell us we have to wear our own private seat belt in our own private property car or they can stop us, search us, ticket us for something else, etc. It's total bullshit, and we let them get away with it. It is simply another excuse they give themselves for bilking us out of our money, and it's our own damn fault. Because we let them. And Buck's right, those seat belt enforcement zones are downright putrid. I saw a seat belt enforcement zone one time where they had set it up at the top of a hill with the sun behind them. I mean come on. When I see how much we seem willing to put up with, I almost have to wonder if we actually *need* something to bitch and moan about. Like a physical need."

"I'm not sure …"

"See, they were at the top of a hill with the sun behind them so that approaching drivers were looking into the sun and couldn't make out the seat belt enforcement zone ahead of time. They couldn't see the seat belt enforcement zone because of the blinding sun, so they wouldn't have time to react and put their seat belts on."

"Wow."

"They can ticket you like $100 for not wearing a seat belt in a 25 MPH zone."

"I really think that it is the very definition of fascism. That is, the seat belt law, the seat belt enforcement zone, and the oppressive implementation of both. I know a guy who got in his car to go three blocks to pick up some milk for Sunday breakfast with the family, never got over 25 MPH, and was ticketed for not wearing his seat belt. Pretty sure that's fascism."

"Our only saving grace is that, for now, we do still have the power to repeal the law. But our most immediately effective power is not in the political machinery. It's in our wallets. We need to dyke the revenue stream. It's time for the non-voting middle-class consumer to step up and harness his ludicrously untapped power. It's time to get back what rightfully belongs to the non-voting middle-class consumer. You want us to keep paying for the whole damn thing? You want us to prop the whole damn thing up? You better give us a break then, pal, is what I'm saying. It would not take that long, given the revenue generation we can dyke."

"We could cure a lot of ills just by staying home."

"Bingo."

"So, 'boycott' is basically what you're talking about."

"Plus, you know what, if they're that concerened about our safety, then how can motorcycles be legal, period?"

"Right."

"Seriously."

"I'm saying I agree with you, Clarkie."

"A guy in the cabin of a car surrounded by a ton of steel *and* with an aribag needs, by law, a seat belt. But a guy on Harley— basically a guy sitting loosely on the top of an 880 cubic-inch engine and a couple wheels—is perfectly street legal?"

"It's all so transparent."

"Buck's right."

They began to dispense themselves across the 9th hole, Buck heading into the pines with Conny trailing him to show him where his ball might be located, Conny pointing Buck towards his ball as it sat on pine straw near one of the hundreds of trees. Blurry headed over to the right side of the fairway. Sweet set his bag down in the middle of the fairway, basking, where he would wait for guys to hit their second shots, Sweet actually looking like the 7-handicapper in the group for the third time on the front-9, a definite record.

While tee shots on the 9th hole hinted at a shift in dominance from Force 2 From Namino, WI, That Is to Sweet and Blurry, second shots solidified it. With his ball sitting up OK in the rough, Blurry took his 5-iron, a favorite of his, put a nice little move on it, caught the flyer lie from the rough and sent it about 185 yds. dead center up the fairway to settle about 160 yds. from the hole. Not bad. Buck refused to just chip out of his situation and tried to take a full swing to advance his ball as far as possible. It ricocheted at least three times off many of the several pines that lay between Buck and the hole and finally came to rest in one of the bunkers across the fairway on the right side of the hole that rarely come into play, normally.

Conny wound up with a great lie in the secondary cut of rough. So good in fact that even though he pulled 3-iron in an attempt to just lay up to somewhere short of the bunkers that sit in the middle of the fairway about 70 yds. out from the green, he caught it absolutely flush and the ball sailed fast and far and bounced hard twice and disappeared. It felt great to have made solid contact again, something Conny had done only once in about his last 8 or 9 shots, but a third shot to the green from a bunker 70 yds. out is a highly difficult shot. Conny had been composing snippets of his Amish vs. Outer Space article here and there over the past 9 holes, and picturing himself with Hootie Johnson over lunch and a beer at Augusta National and laughing about how they would tell large sponsors to fuck off and how appreciative Hootie was of Conny's efforts and how Hootie, too, has been thoroughly disgusted by the amount of commericals during golf broadcasts, *I mean, there's no time-out during golf and yet they inflict the same if not more, probably more, commercial interruptions than any other game that does have time-outs* Hootie would say in his almost incomprehensible Georgian drawl. Conny had been wondering what it would look like for each car on the tollway to have four persons in them, in each and every car during the hours of 5 AM–10 AM and 3 PM–7 PM, M-F, or what it might look like with no cars on the road at all. He wanted so much to take part in these things, but he could not bare losing, especially to some of his best friends.

Sweet, however, was in total command.

Sweet's second shot on 9: Sweet not only knew exactly what he had to do, but knew that if he did it, he would be in the driver's seat as far as front-9 pacts were concerned. The driver's seat for Sweet not necessarily meaning that he could inflict pacts on other guys, but that he could at least avoid his own obligations. This was the "driver's seat" to Sweet at this point because he had been down to Buck, Conny, and Blurry the entire front-9, and tying the score would feel like "victory" then. What he had to do was think about nothing but taking his 6-iron, the very one he had been smoothing for like a half hour straight before the round, the very one he had been creating a small brown radius with over on the range, the range, which was in sight now and which was bringing back really great memories for Sweet. So all he had to do was not waste any time, pull that 6-iron, and smooth one up to about 95 yds. from the hole, which would then be a perfect full-swing sandwedge into the green for him. Clark Bar set his bag down, pulled 6-iron, took one look up the hole from behind his ball, stepped up over the ball, ass perfect and outlined in the color of sunlight meeting fairway. He took one look at his target, brought his eyes back on the ball, waited one click, then released. The result was better than any from the range. Just a really nice low-riser with that second booster propulsion, slight draw on it, and landing softly dead-on, fairway, 95 yds. out.

Having spreadsheeted pacts for the front-9 and the back-9, and surprised that he had actually gotten that far, Conny started laying out pacts for the third portion of the highly intense Nassau—the total-18.

"Buck, if you lose to Sweet for the total-18, you have to repeal the seat belt law." Conny's timing may have been a little insensitive just then, but other guys could not know the raging dissonance going on inside his head.

"Um, OK." Buck was furious at receiving one of the most challenging pacts yet and while on his way to a real trouble shot from the fairway bunker.

Buck's approach shot on 9: Finding that his ball was sitting up nicely and on a slightly uphill lie, Buck felt he had a chance to actually get this ball to the green. He took a 4-iron from 182 yds. and made excellent contact, not picking the ball cleanly as you might see a lot of the pros do in this situation, Buck having that natural slap shot. Missing the lip of the bunker in front of him by what Sweet described as "the hair on a frog's ass," Buck's ball did fly rather torque-mindedly and carried the 182-yd. distance, but into the greenside bunker on the right, to which each of the other guys voiced their own version of something like "Man, this hole sure is no day at the *beach*," or "It's a *beach* of a hole, indeed," etc.

"Sweet if you lose to Blurry for the total-18, you have to learn to play jazz percussion."

Guys were settling around Blurry's approach shot. As they did, it had become concurrently telepathically apparent that no one wanted to lose as they stood in the middle of the 9th fairway about 160 yds. from the hole. It had become apparent that Conny had lost all neutrality. It had become apparent that Sweet did indeed want to avoid any and all obligations, expenses-paid trip to Puget Sound or no. It had become apparent that Buck's euphoria would not be ultimately attained unless he was to come out a winner, and that coming down from losing could take weeks. It had become apparent that Blurry was without his cell phone, not due to happenstance, but that it had been a steely, calculated plan to play without it, and that it was paying off. This became even more apparent after watching Blurry take a 6-iron from 162 yds. and put what looked to be a well-oiled move on it, depositing the ball near the center of the green about 25 ft. right of the pin.

"Very nice, Tom."

"Don't count Tom Blair out."

"Not ever."

They made their way up the 9th fairway, about 70 yds. to cover before they came to where Sweet and Conny were located near each other. The wagers were concrete for them as they walked now; there was nothing ethereal or ephemeral about them then.

"Blurry, if I lose to you for the total-18, I have to campaign for the elimination of fear-based television."

"So, you'd campaign for the elimination of television."

"OK, the problem with this one, Conny, is that people want to watch that shit. People may not want to wait for half an hour just to pay tolls especially when they have no proof of where the money goes, for it certainly is not reflective in the condition of the roads themselves, and people may not want to be forced by law to wear their seat belts because it coddles them like children, and stupid children at that, but people *do* want to watch that shit. And as often as possible."

"It really seems as though they simply can't get enough paranoidal crime drama."

"Or hyper-sensationalized political debate. Also paranoidal."

"Or people eating bugs and feces."

One of the guys said "paranoidal" again.

"Don't you think it's a shame about television?" Blurry had decided his 6-iron to 25 ft. away on the green was quite stellar now that he was copping a bit of a buzz. "When we watch television today, we basically invite *most* of the worst shit life has to offer right into our very own living rooms. Why would we do that?" He sang a refrain or two from "*That's Entertainment*," tipping his hand to the level of his buzz-copping.

"I mean, I was watching the British Open on Sunday morning with my kids and my grandma, the kids' great-grandma, and it's 10:00 AM on Sunday morning and we're watching these guys play their hearts out on one of the most beautiful golf courses in the entire world, and every 3.5 minutes there's either a commercial for erectile dysfunction or a pop-up ad to show what kind of extremely violent paranoidal crime drama one can tune into later that night. This is placed at the forefront of these guys playing the British Open at 10:00 AM on Sunday morning in front of my family, including my grandma."

"Conny's right."

"So, we're dyking the revenue stream on this one again?"

"Oh yeah."

"Nobody watches whatever it is they want taken off the air?"

"No more ass-bearing crime dramas?"

Sweet's approach shot on 9: The amount of confidence Sweet had standing over his approach shot from 95 yds. out in the middle of the fairway would be hard to measure exactly. One could look at him to see that there wasn't a single wrinkle in his forehead or in the cleavage of his eyebrows or around his mouth, and that in fact he may have even been fashioning the faintest smile. Sweet did not change a thing from his pre-shot routine for the smooth 6-iron that got him to this point. Even though the guys were huddled around him as an audience, Clark Bar simply pulled sandwedge from his bag, took one look from behind, addressed his ball, took one look at the target, eyes back to ball, one click, and fired. Taking the kind of beaver pelt (divot) like the pros do on TV to create spin, Clarkie's ball took aim on an area about 8 ft. to the right of pin, bounced once, then grabbed the green and sucked back a bit, maybe 10 ft. short-right of the hole. He would be going to school on Blurry's putt.

"Nice, Clarkie."

"Pretty."

"I know it's not raining, and yet I seem to feel the need for an *umbrella*."

Guys then huddled around the bunker that held Conny's ball. Conny had walked off the yardage from the 100-yd. marker to his ball. It measured 74 yds. to the middle of the green.

Conny's approach shot on 9: A bunker shot from this distance is considered by many to be the most difficult shot in golf. Conny did not have a systematic way of approaching this shot; that is, he didn't really know how to play it. The one thing Conny did know was that he did not want to scull it into Blind Creek behind the green. And it's just real hard to go into the successful execution of a shot you already know nothing about with your primary thought-train being "don't scull it into the creek," especially when that thought occurs at both the top of your swing and then again just before impact, which it did for Conny and which caused him to hit almost two inches behind the ball. The ball then left the bunker quite lifelessly, travelling about 30 yds., and surprisingly so at that.

"Toughest shot in golf, Con-dola."

"Be glad you're still safe."

"I've seen you get up and down from 35 yds. It's not like it's never happened before, Bro-dy."

They were all lying 3, but advantage Sweet.

The practice green, clubhouse, and range were saturated with guys by the time Conny, Buck, Blurry, and Sweet approached the 9th green. And large pockets of them were becoming onlookers. It's not too odd for guys to watch golfers approach the 9th green for something to do while waiting to tee off, but there were more than usual doing this on July 28, 2003, and with specific focus. One of the major throngs of spectators had been forming around Marti Lynn Morley, who was loading up her cart again between the clubhouse and the practice green and serving from her cart as well, which, though it wasn't absolutley clear, did not seem to be the main reasons for guys to be gathering around her. In other words, it appeared as though the biggest pocket of spectators was gathering around Marti Lynn not because she is Marti Lynn and with all the beer, but because she seemed to be pointing towards Conny, Buck, Blurry, and

Sweet as though to say "See, here they come" or "See, there they are." Occassionally it looked like she was saying "See, I told you." Marti Lynn pointed with her head because her hands were busy. Small pockets of guys would break off from the large one around Marti Lynn, and they would continue to watch Conny, Buck, Blurry, and Sweet intently. This did not escape the attention of that foursome as they came up to the 9th green.

The 9th green felt like it was floating. Chances are, with pacts and money both hanging in the balance and with a large gallery scrutinizing them, it was this foursome that was floating, and anything that came in contact with their feet, including the 9th green, latched on to their floating nature. Conny's 4th shot from 35 yds. out had come to rest about 15 ft. to the right of the hole where he would be putting for par, and Buck's shot from the right-hand bunker came up about 18 ft. short on the same line for par, both sandwiched between Blurry's 25-footer and Sweet's 10-footer, each for birdie. Basically, there were four balls taking the same line to the hole from one side. Sweet would get to watch the first three putts, he would get to go to school on three putts, almost assuring him of configuring the correct line. It would simply come down to the purity of his stroke. Something to keep in mind is that Sweet has 3-putted from 10 ft. before. Everybody has. Everybody in this foursome. Everybody watching in the gallery. Everybody has 3-putted from 10 ft. before.

Blurry's putt on 9: Blurry would be first to putt. The combination of playing well and non-cellularity had him secreting aurae. Blurry was flat out positive, man. What other guys couldn't recognize at that particular moment was that Blurry was going through a catharsis, which, that's no small thing to have happen in front of your semi-regular Sat. morning foursome, much less a full-blown gallery. Luckily, it was happening inwardly the catharsis was for Tom, as opposed to the outward brand of catharsis that can sometimes prove to be rather embarrassing in its telling.

As Blurry lined up his putt from behind, his first thought happened to be about an article he had just read in the *Chronicle* called "Law Enforcement Bears Down on Cell Phone Distraction While Driving: 40% of Cell Phone Revenue on the Line." Blurry did not have the time nor the inclination just then to delve as deeply into this catharsis as he would have liked, but he was damn-well realizing that the cell phone had been a bane of *some* kind; after all, here he was putting for birdie on the 9th hole to shoot a 39 on the front-9 at Triple-the-Pines, non-cellular. Then, Blurry did something that proved to himself the depths of his character as it was being brought into stark relief in this non-cellular kind of solitude—he only thought about *score*. The blocking out of everything that hung in the balance and the true focus on the single task at hand proved to Tom that he did indeed have the kind of mental fortitude necessary to compete with anybody. And he stroked his putt. However, as soon as the ball left the face of his putter, Tom could not fight off the thoughts that, were this putt to fall, not only would 1) Conny have to begin work on his Amish vs. NASA article series and 2) Buck his D-CODE program for helping co- and co-co-dependents to hide in domes, but 3) an $32 umbrella would be a done deal, and 4) Sweet would have to make his birdie putt in order to avoid the obligation of starting a common sense parenting prgram based on the somewhat Victorian influence of those who raised the WWII generation. Blurry's ball took a very good line toward the hole and with excellent speed, but as it reached about 5 ft. in front of the hole, Tom realized it was breaking left more than he planned, and deep down Blurry thought that if he could've just kept the thoughts of winning at bay for a little longer, maybe the putt would've had a better chance, though he wasn't at all sure why that would be necessary for the putt to fall. It was just an instinct he had. His ball did end up close enough to the hole for the rest of the foursome to concede the remaining putt though, and Blurry walked away with a par. Voices from the gallery could be heard with a cumulative "Nice try." So much so that Blurry looked over towards the practice green, where some guys waved to Tom and he waved back, surprised.

Buck's putt on 9: Buck would be second to putt. Normally, a guy who was putting with the consequence of having to run for city council on the line, for example, while a hundred people looked on would serve that guy would as a kind of barometer for what it's like to try to putt under the most intense pressure of that guy's life. But not so with Buck. Between his own innate bravado and a fourth really large Old Style he had apparently stashed in his bag during their last rendezvous with Marti Lynn, Buck would not only serve as a poor indicator of "pressure," he did indeed relish the situation. As Buck stood up from lining up his ball, some thoughts from spectators could be heard, though not completely understood; Buck, in a very private place in his mind, took them to be doubts. In another even more private place, Buck knew he did not want to make the effort of campaigning for Carlsburg city council. *What if they do background checks?* probably the first thing that he considered, the second being whether anybody on city council likes to get high. As Buck stood up to his ball, his bravado and beer breath both strong now, he realized that if he made this putt, he would be pact-free regardless of what other guys did with their putts. He took his putter back with one thought: *keep your head still.* This did allow the putter to make excellent contact with the ball. However, a misread on his part started the putt too far out to the right, Buck overcompensating for Blurry's earlier line that broke left well in front of the cup. Buck's ball never really threatened the hole, but it did come to rest within concession distance. He was in at bogey. He thought he heard a gallery member say "Told you so" to another, though he couldn't say from what general direction.

Conny's putt on 9: Conny was third to putt. Whereas Blurry and Buck's putts were not considered "realistic" due to their distances, Conny's was realistic. He was 15 ft. away. As he surveyed his putt from different angles, he could swear he was hearing Marti Lynn Morely say "If he makes this, he breaks 40" and "I'm not sure what that would inflict on the other guys, but it's pretty heavy-duty" and Conny thought about whether he's ever heard Marti Lynn use the words *inflict* or *heavy-duty*. He decided not to consider this too in-depth though. Conny and Sweet were the only ones left with potentially pact-inducing putts now. Sweet, however, did not suffer from Conny's internal tug-of-war between winning the bet but also wanting to improve the Masters and the Earth. Sweet did not hold Buck's sincere curiostiy at how local gov-ernement works, particularly as to whether any of those offi-cials likes to get high, which in a not completely indirect way is still a vested interest in how local governement works. These were not Sweet's concerns, and neither was the raising of today's children by using Victorian ideals instead of pre-scription drugs, nor was the saving of Girl Scout Island. It was not like Sweet was unreadable, the way Blurry had been all day while floating on another plane of non-cellular explo-ration. That is to say that the guys did not have to guess at what Sweet's desires were; he wanted desperately to avoid pacts and his stellar play over the last few holes was driven by this singular goal, which a tie would accomplish as easily as a win would. Sweet did not care about winning. Tying was fine here. But Conny? Conny's mind was in a ruckus. Conny had grown to love the prospect of his own obligations, but he sim-ply could not face losing in order to enact them, God damn it all to hell. And what this did, as Conny stood over his putt, what this did, this final confirmation that he could not pur-posely lose, this lit Conny on fire with competitive determi-nation. So he stood over his putt, conflicted but not in a way that promoted tantalizing neutrality because Conny remembered something important: All he really wanted was to break 40 on the front-9 of Triple-the-Pines. This was the first time since approaching the 1st tee that he had thought so intently about *score*. He thought that shooting or breaking 75 would, for some reason, be ten times easier if he were to shoot 39 on the the front than if he were to shoot 40. With score on his mind, Marti Lynn Morely in his ear, and in front of a gallery, Conny stood over his putt trying to decide on its line, wanting only 39. Conny's knees and lumbar were being consumed by an electric fire, and the zinging ashes shot up through the rest of Conny, where his cranium attempted to build a wall of protection. He looked up and down the line to the hole several times, zeroing in on it between Blurry and Buck's missed putts. He imagined the ball taking the line and falling decidedly into the hole. Conny stroked the ball and watched it start out on the exact line he had portended until it quite suddenly ran out of steam, as so many putts are want to do, inexplicably it can seem, the ball starting to droop 3 ft. in front of the cup, dropping dead at 2 ft. away but directly on line. Conny had considered "line" so fastidiously that he forgot about "speed," and it made Conny want to quit the game as soon as possible, in all seriousness.

Sweet's putt on 9: Sweet was last to putt. What it meant for Clark Sweet to be putting for birdie on the 9th hole with this very realistic opportunity to shoot 39 while a gallery watched can't be measured in the way that we as humans like to measure things, no matter how broadly. "Measurement" is not something that could be applied to what Sweet was feeling just then, maybe because its amount was not finite, nor did it have structure. What Sweet was feeling had no limits. It couldn't even be relegated to "on a scale, 1–10." And the rest of the foursome counted on this to be Sweet's downfall, this hitherto unexperienced and limitless emotion. They hoped it would overcome Sweet, and then make his hands shake badly. At this point, Sweet was one stroke up on the other three men. He could two-putt and tie and avoid any obligations. But birdie … Well, here's what a Sweet birdie would mean:

1) Sweet would have beaten each man by one stroke on the front-9, the pivotal part of the beating taking place in front of a gallery, and

2) Conny would have to begin his campaign for continuing commerical-free Masters tournaments, intense daydreams about conversations on that subject with Hootie Johnson held on the premises of Augusta National probably being the first order of business, and

3) Buck would have to initiate a local ju-co scholarship, taking on the judging of application essays and with no small sense of empowerment, and

4) Blurry would have to develop new and intriguing ways to get people excited about recycling, the rotting of the Earth not being motivation enough especially given the escape option space travel affords, and

5) an umbrella for Sweet and Blurry, which means

6) a garnering of $32 on this hole and a pulling ahead by $19 in the Scotch game, nothing to sneeze at.

Though he had been hot the last few holes and was staring down a birdie putt from only 10 ft. away, Sweet had kind of a problem here; his goal was to avoid, not to win, and it was something he could not convince himself to overcome no matter what the reward for winning. In a place that was too deep down for Sweet to "reach" and, hence, control in himself, he knew that 2-putting here for par, tying everybody, and avoiding his own pacts was equal to/as good as making this birdie putt. Sweet knew, even after watching three putts take the same line as his impending birdie putt, Sweet *knew* he would not be approaching his 10 ft. birdie putt with intent to win, but with intent to make damn sure he did not 3-putt, it being important to remember that Sweet has 3-putted from 10 ft. before just like everybody, everybody else has. He knew that, were the putt to fall, Christ in a pair of Foot-Joys, it would most likely be by pure luck. Sweet knew he was OK with this, and stood over his putt that way. This seeming indifference between whether he made birdie or par should not be mistaken for that brand of tantalizing neutrality that Conny was lucky enough to experience throughout the first 6 holes or so; Sweet was not neutral here. He really was not OK with taking on any pacts for any amount of time, as Conny might have been. True, either a birdie or a par would be fine, but they were both in an intense, hard to measure effort to avoid things. Three-putting in front of an unprecedented gallery and subsequently taking on common sense parenting, consuming only the most immediately biodegradable things, and planting water lilies around Girl Scout Island was on Sweet's mind, which, that's not going to leave any room at all for soothing neutrality. And there was one other thing; Sweet was perfectly fine with 40. A 40 would be well within his oft ridiculed 7-handicap as opposed to, say, the 46 he shot on the front side three days ago. Sweet loved the idea of the glory associated with making his birdie putt, but he could in no way overcome his satisfaction in relinquishing to par. So Sweet putted, unable to feel his arms for the most part. His hands were shaking, he was completely overwhelmed, and he found out that the hitherto unexperienced and limitless emotion he had been feeling was in fact fright. Yet somehow Sweet's putter made decent contact with the ball. Golf has an occasional forgiveness this way, and it's probably responsible the occasional forgiveness is for about 65% of the golfers who continually return to the game. During the 10 ft. the putt had to cover, everything did become hushed, even birds. Every eye at Triple-the-Pines watched Sweet's putt. Every mouth was shut. So, so rare. It rolled as purely as any putt you'll see, certainly as purely as any other putt hit by that foursome so far that day. As soon as Sweet saw this, it actually made words appear to Sweet's mind the way that "stars" will appear to the boxer who just took one square to the nose, those words being *Please. I want it*. And after reading the words in his mind, they offered one last charge the words did so as to look like lightning, then dissipated just as quickly. Sweet was blinded by desire, quite literally, and he was just lucky that the lightning-words dimmed in time for him to see what the ball actually did. Which, as the ball rode the break that had been on display three times before, it headed directly for the middle of the cup. Buck did not want to hear the little echo, and became semi-blinded himself by rage. Conny was simply devoid of sensation by then. Blurry couldn't believe he had played as well as he had, sacrificed his cell phone, and might still be held accountable for innovating new and exciting ways for the exploding population to recycle their shit. As the ball reached the front of the cup, each man had to watch. They couldn't help it. And the ball looked to be rolling over the front edge of the cup, it *did* roll over the front edge, and dissappeared as gravity would deem fit. However, then, as quickly as the ball had gone asunder—actually maybe more quickly than that—the cup spit the ball right back out at Sweet. It did a 180, almost totally submerged, and got spit out. It was like *What?*

Maybe the ball was never truly totally submerged, but every eyewitness from that day will tell you that more than half the ball was in that hole. Way more, actually. It had indeed disappeared. But somewhere in the modest depths of the hole on the 9th green, gravity and the edge of that hole, which is kept as sharp as possible by Phil Black and his crew as are all the holes at Triple-the-Pines so that there is not an ounce, not a fraction of forgiveness, somewhere in that hole gravity and a golf hole split hairs and spit the ball out. The gallery gasped. And they're not exactly the gasping types. Sweet was struck again, the air knocked out of him. The other guys were simply dumbfounded, numb, though they've seen this very thing happen before, and more than once.

Walking from the 9th green towards the clubhouse also means walking towards Carlsburg itself, towards the east side of Triple-the-Pines with Carlsburg waiting outside the bush and Triple-the-Pines behind you now. It was indicated Carlsburg was by that pounding kind of hum that jackhammers, trucks backing up and beeping, large things being unloaded, sirens, and constant traffic can make together especially as they heighten, and they were all heightening at 11:52 AM, July 28, 2003. The guys looked back into the 9th fairway to make sure they had been keeping good pace and saw that Tommy Sheehan's group had not gotten to their approach shots yet, so pace had been well maintained despite a second playing of the 7th hole out there.

Around the practice green and Marti Lynn's beverage cart, there was Brian Hillquist, who was often confused for being Mark Soderquist, though for some reason Mark was never confused for being Brian. Brian took time to interrupt his putting practice to wave over to the foursome as they made their way through the crowd. He had been part of a pocket of onlookers. The foursome were confused as to which one of them Brian may have been waving to, but they seamlessly waved back anyway; 9 holes together has a way of putting four people in syncronicity that way sometimes. Brian had a pretty bad putting stroke but he hit his low irons fairly well and he loved being outside. Conny thought how strange it was, given how often Brian does play, that they hadn't been paired up to play together more often. Mike O'Brien leaned on his putter with one hand, which left his other hand free to make wild gesticualtion while chatting with Stan Frank, Dan Primrose, Jim Pease, and Arlen Frank about something that seemed to recently involve screwing and then unscrewing something, the unscrewing of which having allowed something else to give way onto Mike's head and then the ground around him, apparently. Mike interrupted his story to wave over to the guys as did the rest of that pocket. One of them yelled over to see how the front-9 had ended up, with palpable curiosity. A couple of them looked over to Marti Lynn Morely in association with this curiosity. Conny, Buck, Sweet, and Blurry continued to make their way through the gallery that had grown so thick. The tail end of Buck's bag accidentally bumped Gregg Provo in the knee and all Gregg said was that he hoped Buck's aim had been better out on the course and by the way how did their front-9 end up. Buck said he owed Gregg a beer for it and Gregg said there's no time like the present and then held his hands out to the beautiful day. He and Buck laughed because Gregg was already holding a beer, though Gregg still waited. Four to five other people standing around Gregg and Buck and Marti Lynn commented that Buck owed them a beer too for one reason or another, some reasons of which included actual promises made by Buck on specific dates to buy those persons a beer, dates being cited, and then they asked how the game stood after their front-9 at that point. Liz Ojstaad and Bertie Wilson, who are so decidedly lesbian that there is simply no room for any tension about that, either between guys and the two women or between Liz and Bertie themselves for that matter, high-fived Blurry as he had slowed to contemplate a beer from Marti Lynn's cart but then realized he was on his way into the clubhouse where they also had beer. Liz said that Blurry had the look of a lifetime round going in his eyes; Blurry's resulting smile couldn't mask the fact. Bertie kind of grabbed Blurry by the back of the neck and shook him like a champ as he made his way through. Liz and Bertie were overheard wondering if Clara Franta would show up to play. Somebody short in the crowd spoke up to find out from Sweet about how long he thought that birdie putt was on the 9th, to which Sweet responded it seemed like it was about an hour long. DeBerry was practically blocking the doorway into the clubhouse, the camaraderie seemed to be actually petting him.

Once inside the clubhouse, the foursome sat loosely in incredible comfort around the two unorganized tables. The temperature was such that they were not sweating from their walk nor were they tightening up from taking a seat. They were perfect, resting, and getting ready. There was commotion in the clubhouse as much of Keefe County had apparently decided this day was too much to ignore, but the two unorganized tables were separate from that; that commotion was at the cash register where Pogo did what he could. Marti Lynn had come in to assist Pogo for a few minutes and she brought the guys hot dogs and beer inbetween working a second cash register. Marti Lynn was not as happy in here. Brightly clothed mostly older men filled the clubhouse and they made a weird hum with an annoying bark here and there. Conny noted the similarity between the sound of old men in close quarters and that of rampaging development, but refused to consider it in depth at that time. A lot of the older men didn't work anymore, but they walked their rounds at Triple-the-Pines, many times to be able to say that they could. Though they occasionally glanced up to see what the older men looked like, the guys took conference at the two tables in relative privacy. Conny still had some pacts he needed to relay before a tee shot could be struck on the 10th hole.

This foursome has come out even like this before. Actually, it's pretty amazing how often that can happen after 9 holes, much less 18, that four people can put that much effort into a round of golf with four completely different approaches to the game and still wind up the same via the scorecard. The front-9 had come out even, and after being either scared shitless, overcome with joy, or overwrought with failure over so many shots and putts, it's not unlikely that the other guys were angry with Conny for inciting them this way. Conny was a little angry with himself, but that was because he had thought of several pacts that could help fulfill his weird Nassau prior to taking the 10th tee, but several hits from that fourth beer in the clubhouse had led him to forget a few, and that really sort of pissed him off.

Conny looked at the "40" across from his name on the score-card, 40 being his score for the front-9, then he looked at the other 40s belonging to his playing partners, then looked out the window where he had a perfect view of the 10th tee, and much of what was beyond there. Conny took measure of the weather and how it was still so beautiful out that a 35 on the back-9 was not at all out of the question; 75 was not out of reach yet, not by any means. Conny really got into it, picturing his back-9. Buck, Blurry, and Sweet each looked at Conny staring out the window and the three of them thought concurrently telepathically: *Conny was the editor of his high school newspaper. He had gone to college to study journalism and English literature and still reads poetry if given some really, really spare time. At 40, he was a real estate appraiser.* They wanted to say something and they didn't look at each other. Instead, Sweet scooped up the scorecard and began to itemize outloud the mistakes he made, especially for a 7-handicapper, as well as the successes he had on the front-9, and exactly where each took place. Buck and Blurry weren't really listening, yet they were still annoyed by Sweet somehow.

Conny was so comfortable that he was able to note it to himself. He was looking out the window at blue sky with a few white clouds and he was sitting in unprecedented comfort with friends who had the ability to read his mind. Having used up pacts for charity golf tournaments, his last resort, he was not sure if he would be able to complete the broad Nassau. As he looked out at the back-9 from his chair in the modest club-house, for some reason he thought about one time during a round in March about three years ago, when O'Royerson said that Triple-the-Pines was "like a cocoon." Conny remembered thinking about arguing that notion with Buck since, in fact, there aren't too many games or things that so fully expose you to the elements for as long a period of time as golf does. And that what you're asked to endure by golf, particularly in Chicagoland, particularly in March, as it relates to naked exposure, is almost the antithesis of a cocoon. But he saw the delight Buck had at being at Triple-the-Pines that very moment and the heartfelt warmth beneath his reddened eyes. Conny figured *Hell. Based on where he came from to get here today, a wide open golf course in 41-degree weather and mud in March could seem like a damned cocoon.* Conny came back to the beautiful day in front of him as Tommy Sheehan crossed the window. Tommy, who knows how to twirl his club like a baton.

978-0-595-41619-6
0-595-41619-5

Printed in the United States
88246LV00001B/42/A

9 780595 416196